THE LAST
RESORT

THE LAST RESORT

UNDERGROUND. PARTY TOWN.

A NOVEL BY
BLACK PATRICK

This is a work of fiction. Satire. Silliness. Any similarities to people sharing the same name as you appear within these pages because the author has a sick sense of humor. Be grateful you may or may not be somewhat interesting to someone somewhere. Don't freak out, it's all going to be okay.

Copyright © 2024 by Black Patrick

All rights reserved. No part of this book may be used or reproduced in any manner whatsoever without permission except in the case of brief quotations embodied in critical articles and reviews.

blackpatrick.com

ISBN 979-8-8692-9440-1

3 5 7 9 10 8 6 4 2 1

Printed in the United States of America.

Published 2024
First edition published 2024.

*And if you hear me talking on the wind
You've got to understand
We must remain perfect strangers*
—*Ian Gillan*

CONTENTS

It Happens   1
1. Hard to Kill   3
2. Wheelbarrow Position   11
3. Martin Tarkenton   21
4. Snake River   33
5. LAX Connect   39

Action   51
6. Day One   53
7. Build It, They Will Die   65
8. Greece/Malta   77
9. Bach in Sylmar   85
10. Finish Line   99

Showtime   113
11. Grand Opening   115
12. Blackmore   123
13. The Bell Tower   129
14. Guy Ferrari   135
15. NDGT   139
16. Ava Academy   151
17. Clown Town   155
18. China Wall   159
19. I Left My Heart In…   163

Booming Business   171
20   The Explosion   173
21   Lizards   179
22   Last Stand   185

Special Guest   191
23   Who Are You?   193
24   President Black Patrick   205
25   The Cabinet   209
26   Helicopters   215
27   TV Show   223
28   Braindrops   227
29   Day Four   235
30   Omaha   243
31   Week Two   255
32   Tale of the Tiger   259
33   Flying Machines   267

Well-Oiled Machine   275
34   Operations   277
35   Why?   281
36   Airship Trip   285
37   Welcome Back   291

About Black Patrick   299

More from Black Patrick   305

BLACK PATRICK

"I'm not a champion in action. Every day."
—Black Patrick

BOOK ONE
IT HAPPENS

1
HARD TO KILL

*S**LAM!*
Fuck. Here we go again.

"Hey, Tiko, how's life?"

"Dude, I spend all day digging holes. As soon as I finish digging one, I fill it, and I have to dig another one."

"I feel your pain. What are you gonna do when you run out of Chinese people to plant?"

"Good question."

"Hey, remember when I asked if I could take a dump in a grave?"

"Of course! Are you ready to do some composting?"

"I think so. Is it okay if I bring a package over rolled up in a carpet or do I need to crate it?"

Tiko advised, "Get thick plastic garbage bags and double bag it. When all those body fluids come gushing out you don't wanna leave a trail."

"Cool, thanks, Tiko. Can I stop by tonight?"

"Sure! I have a couple of extra holes so we can use one for your landlord."

"We should invite some goth chicks."

"No doubt. I'll call a few. I have a waiting list a mile long. Chinese goth chicks."

"No way!"

"Way," Tiko said. "I just slaughtered a pig, so we can have a goth luau. Ghost pepper pulled pork."

"Perfect."

"Are you sure she's actually dead? Psychopaths are hard to kill."

"She's dead. Her neck snapped. I think her head might fall off."

"Here's what you do. Fold the head over into her chest and use some duct tape or Liquid Nails to keep everything secure. I had a head roll down the hill onto the freeway once. The news reported a dog ran across the freeway and 'the dog' went flying in the air when a little sports car nailed it and launched it into orbit."

"Nice."

"It just so happened a chihuahua was found running alongside the freeway and everybody was amazed he survived the rocket ride."

"I am in awe of your majesty, Tiko. Should I rent a wood chipper so you don't have to deal with a future Vietcong zombie hooker situation?"

"No, we're good. If you can pick up a big bag of styrofoam peanuts and some diesel we'll make napalm and nuke her corpse."

"Sounds good. Need anything else from Staples?"

I'd spent a fortune on bleach and paper towels since I installed a stripper pole in my apartment. The beauty of living in a high-rise building is everything can be flushed down a toilet—thank you, gravity. Tory requested the spinning-type exercise apparatus when I leased the apartment from her. All I know is, that her neck was twisted upside down and inside out so I tried to fix it with a few good whacks from my bass guitar and that didn't seem to help. When that didn't work I stomped on her throat a couple of times and she didn't wake up. I remembered seeing a TV show once where a paramedic made a patient breathe through a paper bag, so I zip-tied a plastic bag over Tory's head and went to get lunch.

STEWART CONFRONTED ME from his elevated perch behind the bar at Coronado's Mexican Gourmet Mexicatessen. Like a bitch.

"Motherfucker, did you call me a cunt?"

"No! Princess, I would never call you a cunt. You're a fucking cunt." Stewart looked confused and dumb, as usual. "A tostada and a tequila, por favor." Watching strippers die always made me hungry.

Stew sent my order to the kitchen and watched his creepy boss over my shoulder as we caught up.

"Were you raised by wolves?" Stew asked.

"Maybe. What the fuck happened to you? I've never seen a guy sell out so fast and so completely."

"Are you calling me a pussy?"

"No! I would never call you a pussy. That would be dishonest. You're a fucking pussy."

"Nice…"

Stew's weirdo of a boss, a knife-wielding loser named Andy, interrupted our mutual admiration conversation situation by screaming, "Are you fucking kidding me? Are you fucking kidding me?" at a hapless vendor attempting to clean a vent of some kind. For me, it was the funniest thing ever. But I didn't have to work at Coronado's every day. Stew was visibly disturbed by the fracas.

"I wish you were my type. Stew. I have about $20 cash. How deep is your love?"

"Funny. Ha ha."

"Stew, you're in the eye of a hurricane. You don't see it. How long do relationships like yours last? Not long. Not that you had much of one, but your identity as a human being is toast."

"I'm happy."

"Of course you are! Look, we have a pool going. We're betting on how long before that bitch kicks you to the curb. Nobody's buying the squares where your marriage lasts more than three years. It's doomed, you're fucked, prepare for a rough landing."

"How do I do that?"

"Line up some exit strategy pussy in advance."

"What kind of pussy is exit strategy pussy?"

"Every kind. Go on the internet and make a list of the categories you're interested in. Amateur, Asian, babysitter, blowjob, casting, choking, Colombian, edging, facial, fisting, gagging, handjob—"

"I see."

"Remember one thing. When you tell them to do it, they will do it."

"Fisting?"

"Especially fisting. The community college students are really into fisting right now. Pay attention. Don't you read *Trends Journal*?"

TAILGATE TIME AT THE BEACH WITH STEWART.

STEWART DIDN'T WANT TO ATTEND THE LUAU with a dozen hot Chinese goth sluts in the Chinese cemetery. I just assumed he had cancer. Stew was kind enough, however, to help me carry the marinating swine from my apartment to the car.

I thanked Stew for his help as I threw a few sheets of Bounce fabric softener in the back of the Prius and, from a place of compassion, asked, "Stew, how long do you think it'll take your wife to get fat again?"

"Good question. It's only been six weeks since the wedding and she's already chunky."

"Estimate a growth rate of four pounds per month. And that's on the conservative side."

Years and years of remedial mathematics classes served Stew well. "So, she'll be a deuce before our first anniversary?"

"Easily. Minimum. You have Tiko's number, right?"

WITH FOUR HOURS TO SPARE before Tiko's luau, I made a side trip to Hyperion Public in Silver Lake. "You look like shit," the proprietor, Shemp, said as I joined him at the bar.

"Have you ever buried a dead stripper?" I asked.

"No comment."

"So, that's a yes."

"It happens. Need any styrofoam packing peanuts?"

"Does Black Patrick like ketamine?"

"You need to be careful with the white drugs," Shemp said. "Stick with earth tones."

"You need to be careful with that wooden propeller over there behind the dart board. We're having a goth luau at the Chinese cemetery in East LA later if you want to come."

"What else are you burying today?"

"I might bury a special part of me in a Chinese goth fashion student. Or two."

"Bring black candles, sage, and a vintage Ouija board."

"Anything else?"

"Rope and duct tape."

"Ahh, vintage duct tape…"

"What's going on here tonight, Shemp? My guess is, it's either bingo night, trivia night, karaoke night, comedy night, or, if there is a God, burlesque night."

"It's burlesque bingo night."

"Thank you, Jesus. Why are bar owners the least creative people on the planet? Every single hipster hellhole around here has the same hokey event nights."

"Do you have a better idea?"

SHEMP PRESIDING OVER BURLESQUE BINGO NIGHT. LIKE A CHAMPION.

"A bunch. Screaming contest night. Cocaine night. Whispering-only night. Sex worker night. Polka night. Backwards pants night. Bathroom blowjob night. Bring your daughter to the bar night. Foreign exchange student night.

British accent night. Hokey Pokey night. Walk This Way night. Three Stooges night. Win-a-Hooker night."

"All great ideas. I'm combining a couple. A week from Monday is Screaming Hokey Pokey Contest Night."

"You're a true visionary, Shemp.

2
WHEELBARROW POSITION

I FINALLY FIGURED IT OUT. Honker was deaf. Honker didn't have ears. In any case, he needed to stop murdering every woman who climbed my slippery stripper pole. I realized he couldn't see the television when a nude woman was spinning around on the pole. However, no high-speed police pursuit of a dangerous criminal wanted for alleged illegal window tint was of more educational or entertainment value than a hot, naked woman on a stripper pole. Ever.

By the time I arrived in East Los Angeles, a distinct funk filled the air in the Prius. A block away from the cemetery gates I spotted Tiko and his spotted dog, Pico, out for a stroll around the neighborhood. The polka-dotted pair got in the car whereupon Tiko said, "Dude! It smells like something died in here."

"I know, I had Tommy's last night." Tiko directed me into the garage where dead body deliveries slid from coroner vans into a disgusting walk-in freezer and UPS trucks dropped off various materials. We unloaded the garbage bag-encased, stiffening carcass of a dead hooker from the rear of Toyota's finest accomplishment and plopped Tory on a wheelbarrow in the wheelbarrow position.

Tiko. On fire. About to be drugged and raped by a creepy man and a "woman" at a bar. Again.

Tiko outlined his burial process in detail. "I dug a new grave this afternoon a couple of feet deeper than usual so we can dump your landlord in, and cover her in a thick layer of lime, humanure, sand, crushed rock, and dirt after we've seasoned the grave."

"What's humanure?" I asked.

"Human manure."

"Gross. Is that how the grave is seasoned?"

"No. Did you bring the diesel and packing peanuts?"

"Yes, I need a beer."

Tiko's refuge at his workplace/home was a remote out-of-sight corner of the Chinese cemetery where a clandestine outdoor living room complete with a tiki bar and an imu lived behind walls of bamboo.

"What time do the ladies get here?" I asked the guy checking the meat thermometer plugged into a roasting underground pig.

"Probably around midnight, Xyla goes to the goth club and brings home all the hot little girls with fake IDs."

"Whoa. I'm not sure I'm okay with that."

"Ha! Says the guy who brought over a dead stripper."

"Why are there so many cop helicopters flying around here? Are the useless pigs in the sky trying to wake the dead so they can re-kill 'em all?"

"Every freeway in LA goes through here, the hospital has a helipad, the sheriffs have a bunch of helicopters, LAPD has a shitload, the CHP has some…"

"What a waste of money."

"I don't think cops are people," Tiko said. "If we can't kill 'em all we should put 'em in a zoo."

"Tiko, that's a great idea."

"Grab another beer, it's time to nuke a dead hooker before the raccoons eat her face off. They go for the lips and the lips first, if you know what I'm sayin'," Tiko was sayin'.

IF THE CHINESE CEMETERY in East Los Angeles is haunted, I know who the haunter is. Inside the boneyard's centerpiece pagoda hangs a photograph of Honker in human form—something I had never seen. Historical documents, photographs, and artifacts displayed in the pagoda depicted numerous ceremonial occasions, I'm guessing. I don't speak Szechuan.

UNDATED HONKER PHOTO HANGING IN THE PAGODA OF THE CHINESE CEMETERY.

AS SOON AS THE CORPSE WITHOUT A SOUL was deposited and compacted, the special sauce—the styrofoam packing peanuts and diesel fuel napalm compote—flooded the bottom of the dead body hole. Then Tiko wheeled out a cubic yard of his lime/humanure/aggregate mixture and a heavy steel plate. With the carcass covered and compacted once again, Tiko applied the protective metal cap and weighed it down with a dozen sandbags.

Tiko said, "Follow me, put these on," as he handed me a pair of airport tarmac-style headphones. We crouched behind a large tombstone as Tiko lit a string on fire. Ten seconds later an explosion shook the ground and lifted the steel plate above the rectangular cavity in the planet into the air about a foot high. Fire shot out from all sides of the gravesite. It smelled like someone was having a barbecue.

"What the hell was that?" I asked Tiko.

"I buried a stick of dynamite in the hole earlier."

Never one to miss an opportunity, I said, "Me too." The dynamite ignited the napalm mixture and caused an explosion nobody heard because of all the freeway and helicopter noise in the neighborhood. "Dude, you can get away with murder here!"

"When the next dead Chinese person shows up, they get to share eternity with a Vietcong whore," Tiko said.

"Tory always wanted to continue sharing holes in the afterlife. Such a shame to see her die like that. I was hoping a cannibalistic serial killer would meet her at the strip club and take her out."

"Did you use the olive oil on the slippery stripper pole trick again?"

"Honker used bacon grease. I think Tory was studying Kabbalah."

From all appearances, Tiko was living large, in my opinion. "Tiko, you live in a cemetery, roast pigs in a hole in the ground, and blow shit up with dynamite. You're living the dream. Tell me about your typical day."

"I wake up, have a cup of coffee, walk out the door, and dig a grave."

"Do you use a Bobcat or something like that?"

"Nope. Just a shovel."

"How did you get this job?"

"I was dating a hot little Chinese goth girl whose dad was on the board of the Chinese Benevolent Association. When she got pregnant, her daddy gave me this job so I could pay for the abortion."

"How romantic."

"That was 20 years ago. Xyla still doesn't know I'm her dad. Watch out. The Chinese goths are fertile."

"Tikoman, we live in the moment."

If I had to rank all of the fiestas I'd ever attended at a Chinese cemetery, I wouldn't know where to start. Nobody wanted the party to ever end, but Tiko made us all leave just because, allegedly, some family wanted to bury their grandmother—a total bullshit excuse. The festivities were just getting started after the second night. Xyla took me back to my place and had barely shed her all-black ensemble when the cops barged in, screaming incoherent and contradictory things. Don't these people go to school, or something, before they're given guns and bazookas and tanks?

My alleged criminal conduct was murder, Xyla was charged with pimping and pandering, whatever that means, I think. As the old saying goes, no body, no crime, so the ignorant and useless pigs would never be able to convict me of anything.

The booking process at the jail was relatively fun, especially the cavity search. I didn't know the jail lined up all of the deputies so you could choose the hot little Latina. My mugshot might not be as awesome as this one:

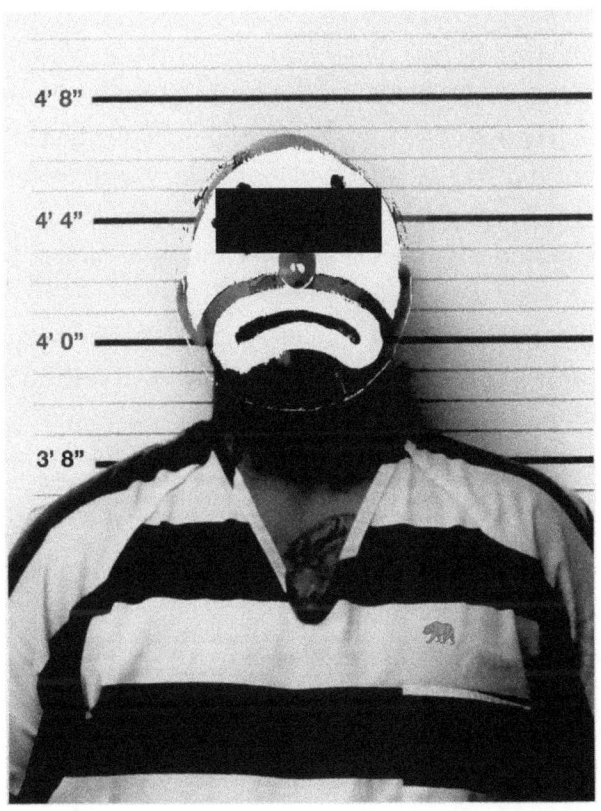

A MUGSHOT HANGING ON THE WALL OF THE "TWIN TOWERS MUGSHOT HALL OF FAME" IN DOWNTOWN LOS ANGELES.

By now, at this age, by all accounts, under any circumstance, I should not be surprised when Honker appears. I should not be surprised he is officially a little person, either. He's a full three inches below the maximum height to be a certified and bonafide dwarf. Now that I know this fact about Honker, when I get out of prison, I'll tell him about the Hungarian guy who was both a dwarf and a giant.

Where do strippers go when they die? Why don't I know that? Did I miss the day in school when all of the important shit was taught? With any luck, I shall travel to the place where exotic dancers dwell post-mortem. Some believe those who lead a useful life are reincarnated as a tree. Sounds boring.

Tiko bailed me out of the Los Angeles County Jail and we retired to a tiki bar with excellent freeway access. "Where's Xyla's mom, Tiko?"

Tiko thought for a moment and said, "She's around here somewhere."

"Kyla named her kid Xyla?"

"Kyla is also Xyla in Chinese."

"Do you ever see Kyla?"

"I come across a piece or two once in a while. I'm a simple man. I'm happy to stay here at the bok choy farm, drink beer, snort ketamine, barbecue, and play in my funk band. Kyla needed more excitement. So I killed her."

"I get it. Most people in your situation would have done the same thing. That's because nobody else on earth lives at a Chinese cemetery, snorts ketamine, plays in a funk band, and digs graves for a living."

"Yeah. I know it looks glamorous from the outside, but it's not. I'm going back to school to become a phlebotomist."

"Why phlebotomy?"

"Imagine yourself in a classroom with all Filipina foreign exchange students majoring in nursing."

"I have. Do you do any organ harvesting here?"

"Once in a while the college brings students here to yank some kidneys or corneas out. I don't know what they do with 'em after that, but I get free tuition."

Xyla and her All-Knowing Eyes

"Have you ever thought about reaching out to the shovel companies for an endorsement deal?"

"I like to keep a low profile. I don't need to see my picture in all the grave-digging magazines to feel successful."

"Dumbfuck, listen. One ad in one Chinese grave-digging trade publication will make you a superstar in China. Like Kobe."

"Fuck that. I hate helicopters. And I don't really wanna be a phlebotomist. What I really wanna do is operate my own cemetery. We're almost full here and I don't wanna start all over again in some other branch of the death industry. I'm the king of the Los Angeles Chinese cemetery industry, anything else I do in the future will be a downgrade."

Believe it or not, my incoherent form of questioning always leads to no good and great things. The dim bulb above my head flickered with a tremendous idea—a 21st-century cemetery built to celebrate life.

"Tikoman, mark my words. We'll build you the coolest cemetery on the planet."

3
MARTIN TARKENTON

Martin Tarkenton figured out how to be awesome a long time ago. Perhaps in another life. Today, he walks around with the old soul demeanor old school people who never went to school like to talk about.

"Black Patrick, you look great!"

"Sorry, Martin, I'm taken. What the fuck's wrong with you?"

"Fever."

"Fever?"

"Yeah, fever," Martin said. "Valley Fever."

"What the fuck is that?" I asked.

"Fever, cough, muscle aches, fatigue…"

Dr. Black Patrick took a seat at The 19th Hole's well-worn bar, ordered four shots of tequila, and wasted no time recommending the following treatment: "Martin, you need drugs and tequila. And get the fuck out of this golf course business bullshit. Golf is for stupid people."

"I'm done with golf. The county is eliminating their exposure to golf. Apparently, there are almost as many incidents of child molestation amongst golf course people as social workers in Los Angeles County."

"That's no surprise."

"That's a good Aerosmith song."

"I think *Chiquita* is their best song."

"I like *Uncle Salty*, from *Toys in the Attic*," Martin said.

"That song sucks. You're a child molester."

Martin took my advice and ordered drugs from the ever-faithful and punctual heroes working for the local cartel. Fifteen minutes after our friend in the red Honda appeared, Martin's potentially fatal fever condition was in remission. "The county's selling the entire property. Some open space coalition wants to buy it so mountain lions can hang out here."

My immediate and uneducated opinion of the mountain lion premise was, "That's a great idea. Especially since there's a park, a playground, a picnic area, 14 baseball diamonds, and a few schools surrounding this place."

"Yeah…"

"And bears!"

"Pic-a-nic basket-stealing bastards."

M ARTIN LED ME ON A TOUR of Sylmar's most depressing golf course. At the operations building he pointed at a giant trash can and asked, "Want one of these?"

MARTIN TELLING HIS WIFE HE'S NOT HAMMERED. AND HE DIDN'T BUY ANOTHER GUITAR.

"A trash can?"
"It's full of golf balls."
"What the hell do I do with a thousand golf balls?"

"Somehow, I know you'll find something to do with a thousand golf balls."

I left Sylmar with a bad taste in my mouth. It may have been the burger. It took me a day or so to connect the dots. Combine the Sylmar golf course with a place for dead Chinese people. And other dead people. And people who will be dead one day.

"TIKO, TELL ME ABOUT YOUR PLAN for a cemetery."

"All I need is ten acres, man. One acre for my house, four acres of traditional gravesites, three acres of composting, natural-style graves, an acre of crypts, and an acre for administrative and operational facilities."

"What will make your cemetery better?"

"Well, first of all, it won't be corporate. None of the bullshit, song-and-dance, buy two get one free. No rules about tombstones. Put in a Washington Monument if you want, I don't care. If you want to have a barbecue next to the funeral ceremony, awesome. If you want a punk band to play while you're burying someone, beautiful."

"What if I told you we can get our hands on 12 acres for the Chinese people?"

"I will kill myself before I move to Orange County," Tiko said.

"Me too. It's not in Orange County."

"Where is it?"

"Sylmar."

"Fuck. That's perfect."

T IKO NEVER CALLED THIS LATE AT NIGHT. "What's going on in Sylmar?"

"Don't talk about this. The spot in Sylmar is a golf course owned by the County of Los Angeles. Nobody plays golf anymore, so the county wants to do something else with it. You need $10 million from the Chinese Benevolent Association. They get 12 acres in Los Angeles County."

"12 acres? $10 million is half the price of a shitty house in San Marino."

"I said $20 million."

"No, you didn't."

"Whatever. They'll probably come up with $40 million, but we can work with $25 million. Tell them we need $25 million and they get 16 acres. We'll build the most badass underground Chinatown the planet has ever seen."

"They need the space. Don't tell anyone, but we're at 96% capacity in East Los."

I knew how to light a fire under Tiko. "The new place has a bar."

"Fuck."

While Tiko worked on the Chinese investors, I hammered out a proposal for the County of Los Angeles with golf course guy Martin.

"The county wants to see a bunch of bullshit about how you're family-friendly, all-inclusive, affordable, creating jobs for people who shouldn't be allowed to leave the house unsupervised, etc."

"So, we need an LGBTQ+ section, a Chinese section, a free section, and an abortion clinic."

"Most of that. You were testing me to make sure I was paying attention. You're the one on drugs with the drinking problem."

"Martin, we're doing all of that but, more importantly, we're doing whatever the fuck we want. We're showing up with a check for $10 million, we're sinking another $20 million into improving the place, and we're paying whatever rate they ask for an annual lease for 99 years. As long as we can do whatever the fuck we want."

"Don't tell me what you're planning to do."

"Here's what we're not going to do. We're not doing the standard cemetery thing—there are plenty of those places already. Do you want to hear what we're going to do?"

"No."

"This will take a minute. Open 24 hours. Like Denny's. Like 7-11. No locks on the gates at Honker Cemetery."

"Oh, no…"

"Tombstone Tuesdays. Brought to you by Tombstone Pizza."

"No."

"People can be buried next to their pets. Spend eternity with your puppy…"

"Jesus."

"A heavy metal section where metal fans can be buried. No posers."

"You'll need a punk rock section, too."

"Done. I'm thinking about a separate Black Sabbath section where people are buried standing up facing a stage with hologram Sabbath dudes. Ozzy. Tony, Geezer, Bill, Ronnie, Ian, Vinny. "

"What about Cozy?"

"Good catch, yes."

"You know, you can bury a lot more people vertically."

"No shit. All we need is one of those post-hole digging auger attachments on the bulldozer, put the dead body in a Sonotube, shove it down the hole, add a little bit of concrete, fill the hole back up, bam. Next!"

"You'll wanna use the Sonotubes with Rainguard."

"Absolutely. We'll have a classical section, jazz, blues, show tunes—"

"Hanz Zimmer?"

"Somebody needs to bury that guy right away."

"Country?"

"No country. Anything but country. We'll do funk, hip hop, Fela Kuti, polka—"

"The Bling Thing."

"Okay. Whatever that is. A bowling alley, electric car charging station, movies, amphitheater for live bands."

"Cool."

"Eight rooms for Airbnb guests."

"Go for it."

"Are you ready for the big one?"

"I'm not your daughter."

"I don't have kids, here it comes."

"My ears are plugged."

"A ghost kitchen."

"You can't do that. A ghost kitchen at a cemetery?"

"Watch."

"A ghost kitchen at a cemetery?"

"We're preserving one hole on the course so golfers can be buried on a golf course."

"We should have a miniature golf course."

"You should be buried in a sand trap when you die."

"I already have one picked out."

"We're turning the pro shop into a flower shop and The 19th Hole into Ashes to Ashes."

"Clever."

"Tiko's caretaker's compound will have a 6,000-square-foot basement with a strip club. Full bar, all nude, dancers start on their 18th birthday. We're calling it The 18th Hole."

"No, you're fucking not. You need to learn about the 1971 Sylmar tunnel explosion. Don't even think about basements around there."

"Okay, we'll build the strip club above ground and call it The Mausoleum."

"That's a great idea," Martin said.

"Parking for tour buses, a recording studio, bungalows for the talent—"

"The talent?"

"Did I stutter?"

"Are you related to Crazy Eddie?" Martin asked. "Your ideas are batshit crazy."

"Martin, fuck you. I'm not Syrian. Every Syrian is a child molester."

"I didn't know that. I knew they were cunts."

"Every transaction with a Syrian is like trading a donkey for a bushel of wheat with those cunts."

"Is that racist?"

"Not when it's true," I responded. "I love the way people in those places claim they're responsible for human evolution yet they've never invented a goddamn thing."

"Everything we think we know is wrong," Martin said.

"Crazy Eddie had a try-before-you-buy policy. Why don't hookers do that?"

"Did Mojo Nixon ever dig up Howlin' Wolf?"

"We need to dig up Crazy Eddie. That fucker partied harder than anyone."

"Why are we talking about Crazy Eddie?"

"Because Crazy fucking Eddie's prices were insane!"

TIKO AND I DECIDED A HAPPY HOUR CONFERENCE AT THE 19TH HOLE with Martin would be a good idea. I'd barely started on my Double Bogey when a weird dude with spiky blonde hair wearing a zebra print ensemble and goofy sunglasses sat down at our table.

"So, how's the body-burying business going, Black Patrick?" Daniel Tiger asked.

"I'm not in the body-burying business, Daniel. Tiko dabbles in that from time to time."

Daniel Tiger swiveled his chair toward Tiko and asked, "So, Tiko, how's the body-burying business going?"

Since business wasn't booming at the Chinese cemetery, Tiko wasn't getting a whole lot of cardio action digging holes for dead people. As he finished the last bite of his low-calorie Birdie Special, Tiko told Daniel, "It could be better, Daniel. Can you drive through Chinatown and mow some old Chinese ladies down for me?"

"Shut up, Tiko," Daniel Tiger said. "I know you clowns are cooking up some kind of deal. I can tell by the look in your eyes and the pajamas Black Patrick's wearing. I want a piece of the action. $10 million and I won't settle for anything less than 5%."

I told Daniel, "Give us a few minutes, Tiger. Grab a bucket of balls and hit the range. Maybe we'll come find you if we can find a reason to not be insulted by your lowball offer. Get out."

None of us had any idea how or why gangster Daniel Tiger knew about our plan to turn a golf course into a cemetery. Martin swore he hadn't said anything to the guy in the red Honda. Afraid Daniel might have planted listening devices in the building, we retreated to Martin's office and communicated via handwritten notes, sign language, and facial expressions. No sensible person would value five percent of our cemetery/bar & grill/entertainment complex at $10 million. But we wanted his $20 million, so we demanded it and we took it.

"Okay, now we have enough money to build Main Street D.O.A.," I told Tiko and Martin.

"What the hell is that?" Martin asked.

"Go to Disneyland. Ours will be the same size, exactly like the Disneyland version except we'll have bars, restaurants, a golf crap shop, burial sales, and Airbnb upstairs."

"We should do a Chinatown, too," Tiko said.

"No. Fuck that. We're putting in a Zankou Chicken with a full bar."

"Which Zankou Chicken?" Martin asked.

"What do you mean?"

"There are two Zankous. One part of the family owns some locations, another one owns the rest. And they don't get along. That probably would have happened to In-N-Out Burger if the whole family hadn't died in that plane crash."

I figured there was no reason to continue to keep secrets from Tiko and Martin. So I asked, "Do you want to hear how we're going to be the very most profitable cemetery in American history?"

Both Martin and Tiko said various versions of no—.

"Tiko, we're burying people standing up."

Professional corpse planter Tiko asked, "How the hell am I gonna do that?"

"Sonotubes," Martin said.

"That'll work."

DANIEL TIGER. ON SAFARI. AT A TRUCK STOP. ON A COMPOSTING TOILET IN THE OUTBACK. A GAY BAR.

AT THE END OF THE DAY, DANIEL TIGER'S $25 million plus the $25 million Tiko extorted from the Chinese Benevolent Association and Martin's excellent credit score convinced the Los Angeles County Board of Supervisors to sell us the golf course. I don't think the compromising photographs and video Daniel Tiger sent the supervisors made any difference—who knows?

4
SNAKE RIVER

As we finalized the purchase agreement with the County of Los Angeles and the government permit and planning hoops were effectively cleared, I boarded an airplane and took a trip to see CPA Chris at his enormous ranch outside of Boise, Idaho.

"Welcome to paradise, Black Patrick," the perfect ten of a supermodel maid said as she beckoned me into the CPA Chris lodge.

Before I could stammer a response to the prototype of a housekeeper most people with penises fantasize about, Chris appeared, shoved a tall, cold can of IPA in my hand, and announced, "We're goin' fishin'!"

And we were goin' fishin'. Chris led me out the back door of his abode down a meandering path through pungent farmland to a terminus at a rustic boathouse. "What the hell is that?" I asked Chris.

"A Thunder Jet. You're driving. I'm too hammered."

Well, there's a first time for everything. The Thunder Jet's operating controls looked simple enough, so I grabbed the steering wheel, pulled back on the throttle, shot out of the boathouse, and almost killed us both. Chris howled with laughter.

"What kind of engine does this thing have?"

"Suzukis! A pair."

Suzuki is the most beautiful word in the English language. A pair of Suzukis is the most wondrous sight imaginable. I'll save that for the next book.

Chris approached a fishing expedition the same way a tremendous American named George Clinton of Parliament, Funkadelic, and *Atomic Dog* fame is alleged to have—with a big bag of joints and a big bag of cocaine.

"Where the fuck are we?" I yelled at Chris over the whine of dual Suzukis.

"The Snake River."

"The Evel Knievel Snake River?"

"Yep. You're like Evel—you almost, almost killed us. I'm a farmer here."

"Who cares? Where are the fish?"

"Give a man a fish, and you feed him for a day; teach a man to fish—"

I walked right into that one. I told the man doubled over crying, "Fuck you, Chris. Fuck you," as I slammed the steering wheel to the left and executed street takeover-style donuts in the middle of the river.

CPA Chris. On fire.
Planning to abscond
with all of our cash.
Like a bitch.

With hooks in the water, I brought up the pertinent business we needed to discuss. "What's the deal with your maid?"

"Who knows?" Chris responded. "She keeps the place spotless, I show up every few weeks, and Fiona is excited to see me."

"Wow. You should have a bunch of places like that."

"I do."

And that was the moment I knew I should have become an accountant.

"How much money do we have left for the design and build of our cemetery?" I asked CPA Chris.

"Not enough," bad news bearer Chris reported, "but I found a way to fix that."

"We don't want any more of Daniel Tiger's dirty money."

"Daniel's money isn't dirty, he's a client. That fucker banks $10 million after taxes on a slow month. He's loaded."

"How?"

"Shampoo. He sells shampoo on TV. Daniel works four days a year and owns a dozen mansions in Los Feliz. He's a celebrity hairstylist, by trade. Hair products magnate, too."

"Fuck me. We all thought he was a drug dealer."

"He's good for a few dozen million more if we need it. But we won't."

"Liquid Death is willing to pay $5 million for naming rights to the amphitheater."

"Chump change. Peanuts," Chris said. "What if I told you we can generate more than $100 million in investment capital?"

"Tell me more, Bernie. I'm in. Who do we have to kill?"

"Nobody. The federal government has an immigrant investor visa program. We need 100 investors to invest $1.1 million, bam, we're flush with cash."

"Fuck."

Armed with new information about the wonders of immigration visas from CPA Chris, I set about finding creative ways to blow $100 million. While Chris scheduled seminars and hookers all over Asia, I spent a couple of days in Boise preparing presentation materials for his travels and concocting great ideas. We hired a general contractor to oversee construction alongside our starchitect, Golden Richards. And we started searching for a landscape director to get some rapid-growth trees in the ground. We were going to need a lot of privacy for what we were planning.

5
LAX CONNECT

CPA Chris, starchitect Golden Richards, and I set up a meeting at an airport-adjacent hotel ballroom with Martin, Tiko, Tiko's new assistant, Xyla, and Daniel Tiger on Chris's way out of town to Asia to raise money. Golden and I met with the three best candidates for the landscaping gig prior. Two of the job seekers were stupid, the third was a goth supermodel named Beth working on her dual graduate degrees in Master of Landscape Architecture and Master of Urban Planning. We hired Beth on the spot. I had seen some of her videos on the internet.

I told Beth, "We need you to handle all of the shit growing on the property—manage the landscaping crew, and the trees, run the flower-selling operation, plant a food forest and manage the farmers' market and produce sales. We need trees in the ground now."

"What's my budget?" Beth asked. "I need $200,000 for trees, a 2,000-square-foot greenhouse, and an assistant."

Evil starchitect Golden Richards lying to the planning commission.

"That won't work," Golden said. "$200,000 might cover a couple of dozen mature olives, avocados, and oaks."

"Yeah, there's no way," I added. "We budgeted $3 million for trees. We want big, gnarly, badass trees looking to party with their tree friends and families forever. The greenhouse is 10,000 square feet and you need to start hiring."

Beth leaped aboard our enterprise, we joined the assembled gang at the hotel bar waiting for the festivities to commence—CPA Chris, Martin, Tiko, Daniel Tiger, and, the love of my life, Xyla. Golden Richards had never met anybody else in our ragtag group, for good reason, and Beth was somewhat appalled by the crew. Except for Xyla—sparks flew between Beth and Xyla. Shots of tequila and appetizers prepared us all for the champagne room presentation in the Commander's Ballroom.

I picked up my pool stick/presentation pointer, slammed it on the conference table, and yelled, "Silence!" The sound echoed throughout the gigantic room as a remote-controlled fighter jet screamed around the room frightening all of us.

"We're doing that," I said, "and a whole lot more!"

I flung the cover page of the presentation printed on giant sheets of paper sitting on the antique easel and informed the gathered elite of our shared destiny:

The Last Resort
    Main Street
    The Ghost Kitchen
    19th Hole
    Chinese Cemetery
    Veterans' Cemetery
    Regular Old Dead People Cemetery
    Columbariums
    Crypts

Catacombs
Chapel
Liquid Death Amphitheater
Golf Hole
Golf Cemetery
Food Forest
Greenhouse
Operations
Cremations
Tiko's Caretaker's House

Then, as the lights in the ballroom dimmed, indoor thunder and lightning struck. Golden's architectural model of the project rose from the floor to awe and inspire us all.

CPA Chris had a plane to catch so he grabbed the architectural model, my Mandarin-speaking goth supermodel girlfriend, and boarded the shuttle bus to the airport after a few more shots at the hotel sports bar. Bye, Chris. And Xyla.

Martin's face showed concern. "What the fuck is Main Street?"

"Wait. You'll see."

Back in the ballroom, the presentation continued via PowerPoint on a projection screen with me wielding a laser pointer. Like a champion.

"Our business: The Last Resort.

"Main Street is the hub. Two restaurants, cemetery sales, a flower shop, a nightclub/venue, and the resort lobby on the ground floor. Hotel rooms on the second floor, suites on the third and fourth floors, and a rooftop pool/spa/club/restaurant.

"The Chinese people get a separate cemetery, the veterans get one, too, and regular old dead people get one—that's where the chapel will be located. The Liquid Death Amphitheater at The Last Resort is for music, movies, and dead people buried standing up. And more.

"And we have a golf section to bury golfers.

"Martin is in charge of everything—golf, cemetery sales, the resort, operations—we all work for him.

"Tiko deals with all of the dead people and the Chinese people. We're building him a kick-ass caretaker's home on the property.

"I deal with the amphitheater and entertainment end of things.

"Beth deals with the living things. She overstocks the flower shop, grows produce for our restaurants, and manages our weekly farmer's market.

"Oh, I left out one thing. The ghost kitchen."

"How the hell are you going to afford all of that shit?" Daniel Tiger asked.

"Chris will bring back enough cash from wherever he has to go to line up enough capital to make it all work. Next question."

Martin was still worried about golf. I hope. "What the hell do I do with only one hole?"

"You make history, motherfucker," I responded.

"I'll need help."

"No shit. You need a food and beverage director, a sales team, a human resources director, someone to manage a 120-room resort—"

Tiko said, "I'm not sure the Chinese Benevolent Association will be okay with all of this."

"We're selling them 20 acres for $1."

"They'll be cool with that."

"Opening Day is 14 months away. That's, essentially, tomorrow. Golden Richards and I will be on site all day tomorrow."

Beth said, "I can be there at 6 a.m."

"Perfect."

"Hey, I just wanna close this by telling you guys we are going to do something that's never been done before. This will be a legendary victory or a monumental failure. The worst thing we can be is average. Fuck that. We go for it. Full fucking blast. Fuck anyone who stands in our way. Success or Hindenburg!"

AT THE HOTEL'S POOLSIDE BAR post-presentation, Daniel Tiger needed details. He sat down next to me, stared into my eyes, and demanded, "Tell me about your five-star resort, Black Patrick."

"It's a 120-room hotel and resort with kick-ass suites. The Presidential Suite will overlook it all. Five thousand square feet of luxurious interior space, a private elevator, its own rooftop pool and beach, don't tell anyone."

"I want it."

"It'll cost you—"

"Silence! I want it."

"Done."

I sent Daniel a Venmo request for the first year's room rental for the Presidential Suite, $3.85 million arrived in our account within an hour. A separate $500 per day resort fee landed in another Venmo account designated for "Jet Fuel" which we regularly tapped for the powerful and necessary narcotics any creative organization requires to change the world.

Martin arrived next with another stupid question: "What the fuck are we doing here, again?"

"We're building the most awesome place to spend eternity the world has ever seen," I responded.

"What about the golf course?"

"Fuck golf. Golf is for stupid people. We're saving the bullshit signature hole for those visor-wearing fucks and charging them a boatload of money to play it. And, if they wanna be buried there in their stupid golf clothes, the burial fee is enormous."

A dejected Martin said, "That doesn't sound like something I can be a part of."

"Didn't I tell you about the 18th Hole?"

"Maybe. What's that?"

"The secret, identical reproduction of, Jumbo's Clown Room in the basement under Tiko's house with 18-year-old strippers."

"I'm okay with the golf thing now."

"Your job is impossible, but we'll have a massive budget, so you can hire an army of people," I told Martin. "The first step, in my opinion, is to hire a badass, creative, acid-tripping, recruiter of a human resources manager to tap into all of the talent at the community college on the other side of the fucking fence. And staff up at The 19th Hole so you have a pool of talent to cultivate and prepare for the day we change the world."

"No problemo."

"We're building a secret underground wine cellar, too, under Main Street. And a speakeasy."

"How do we get away with that?"

"Our contractors build all of the freeways and shit around here," I told Martin. "The hole's dug, the concrete's poured, all of the secret underground chambers are done in a few hours. If they need more time a freeway overpass crack is discovered or a gas leak happens somewhere in Sylmar to divert the inspectors."

"I'm worried about basement things," Martin said. "What about the Sylmar Tunnel Disaster of 1971?"

"Please. Those fuckers want us to believe Lockheed was 200 feet underground digging a water tunnel? What a fucking joke. 200 feet? Here? For water? Four months after a huge earthquake? Why?"

"For water."

"A defense contractor building a tunnel 200 feet underground? Please. It doesn't add up. Something smells bad."

"Methane smells bad. I grew up in Modesto. There are a lot of black helicopters flying around the golf course, sometimes. And that tunnel entrance is not exactly hermetically sealed."

"Shocking. I guarantee you—dig 200 feet under anywhere and you're running into evidence of an ancient civilization."

"How much money are we going to make doing this?" Martin asked.

I showed him the Venmo deposit from Daniel Tiger. "The resort has 120 rooms, one suite is already sold out for the entire first year we're open."

Tiko was all good with whatever, he and the ghost of Kyla were already planning to spend most of their time shopping for window treatments for the caretaker's home. "We'll need a freezer," he said.

"You'll have a few. Did I tell you about the strip club under your house?"

Tiko ignored my question, like a bitch, and suggested, "Let's pre-vault the whole Chinese place."

"What does that mean?" I asked.

"We plant the concrete vaults in advance, while the excavators are around."

"What's a vault?"

"It's the concrete box the casket goes in. A plain concrete box with a lid, that's it. They're about $2,000 each. If we plant 5,000 in advance we'll save a lot of time and money in the future. We should be good for five years, at least."

"Fuck that. We're not spending $10 million on concrete box bullshit. We can build our own forms and pour our own concrete boxes and lids for 25% of that. Great work, Tiko, you just saved us millions. Any more bright ideas?"

"Hookers."

"Tiko, you're a goddamned genius. Bring it! Every fucking idea. Bring it!"

AFTER OUR MEETING, Tiko and I headed to the world-famous Rainbow Bar & Grill on the Sunset Strip to get hammered and secure a deal to open an identical Rainbow twin on Main Street.

The third-generation proprietor of Rainbow Bar & Grill had a better idea for a licensing deal than I did. "Instead of

$100,000 and $5,000 every month, give me $300,000 right now and it's a done deal."

"Right now, right now?" I asked.

"Right fucking now."

"Deal."

Daniel Tiger arrived an hour later with three bricks, another mission accomplished.

THE ORIGINAL RAINBOW BAR & GRILL - SUNSET STRIP.
I MISS THAT WOMAN WHO TOLD ME ABOUT THE TIME
SHE BLEW MARILYN MANSON THERE.

BOOK TWO
ACTION

6
DAY ONE

DAMN. THE WHOLE TEAM WAS ON FIRE and ready to rock in Sylmar at 6 a.m. the next morning. Martin's 19th Holers were on the griddle and pouring black gold to golfers and assembled geezers.

Tiko said, "I drove a golf cart all over this place. Fuck yeah. It's money in the bank, motherfucker."

Martin asked, "How much money do I get paid for all of this bullshit here?"

"How much do you want?" I asked.

"$5,000 a week and a Tesla."

"We won't make any money for a year, at least," I told Martin.

"We generated $3.85 million in revenue yesterday."

"Oh, yeah, I forgot about that. What's your Venmo?" I sent Martin $260,000 of Daniel Tiger's money for the first year and told him to buy his own goddamned Tesla. Boy, was he pissed when we bought Beth a Cybertruck.

Beth had a plan and a list and was on a mission to make shit happen. After breakfast and a quick golf cart tour of the property, Beth told me she wanted the water features scooped out to be much deeper and we needed to buy as many of the 14 baseball diamonds surrounding the property as we could.

"Done," I agreed. "Fuck baseball."

Then Beth hit the road and became Southern California's best wholesale nursery customer since Walt Disney in the 1950s.

BECAUSE OUR LIVES DEPENDED ON IT, we slammed square pegs into round holes and, like champions, conquered the misery of the planning and permitting process. Just enough to get the party started. We knew we were looking at massive battles with geniuses in the government and busybodies in the neighborhood going forward. Fuck those people—it's better to beg for forgiveness later than ask for permission now. We do what the fuck we want.

The day after the last round of golf concluded a convoy of trucks delivered shitloads of heavy equipment and megatons of materials to the site. Then the earth moved under our feet. Starchitect/Designer Golden Richards's years as an Imagineer at Disney and an architect at Gensler prepared him to kick ass all over the place the cool people would spend eternity. Martin kept The 19th Hole operating to feed construction workers and his alcoholism when he wasn't asking me, "What the fuck's going on around here, again?"

"You'll see, Martin. You'll see."

CPA CHRIS TOLD ME THE IMMIGRATION visa posse needed us to host a groundbreaking party as a photo opportunity so the visa applicants would have evidence of their involvement in the project. Never ones to pass up the chance to throw a party, we invited everybody we could think of to witness the shovel ritual and join us for a barbecue after.

THE LAST RESORT'S GROUNDBREAKING
GROUNDBREAKING CEREMONY. BEFORE THE NAPALM
AND HOOKERS.

A COUPLE OF WEEKS LATER, BETH INVITED ME on a tree-buying expedition. "We're gonna fuck some shit up," Beth said, on our way down the freeway to a tree farm near San Diego.

"How?"

"Beavers."

"Xyla gets back from Taiwan in a couple of weeks."

"Not that kind of beaver, you pervert. We're planting beavers in the hills above the cemetery and stocking the golf course ponds with fish," Beth announced. "I'm a motherfucking rewilder."

"Can you rewild Xyla when she gets back?" I asked Beth. "All people are beautiful, so long as they are wild."

"I'm not a hippie. I'm not a tree-hugger. I'm not a fucking vegan. I'm a rewilder."

"We bought four baseball diamonds yesterday. You can rewild that shit right now."

"Fuck! Great! Team sports are for dumbfucks."

"Beth, you are on fire, 24/7."

"That's what my partner says."

"What's his name?"

"They are named Carlito Bandita."

"They?"

"Carlito is transitioning, they uses the 'they' pronoun."

"What does that look like?"

"If Carlito's on all fours and I move his junk out of the way while I'm rim—"

"No! Not that! I was asking metaphorically. The relationship part. What does a relationship with a they look like?"

"Oh, the relationship part is the same deal. Bitches are bitches. What are you gonna do?"

Beth was full of surprises, "We adopted four poopers," she said.

"Poopers? What are poopers?" I asked.

"Two sets of sibling poopers. We need poopers to manage the lawnmowers and help protect the chickens."

"If you say so."

"Four Australian shepherd puppy people."

"Four fucking puppies? That's awesome! You know there's no way I won't be spending every minute of every day with those little monsters. For the next 20 years."

"Don't be a little bitch, Black Patrick. I felt that way when I met Carlito."

"Yeah, but Carlito's a human. We're talking about puppies here. Puppies!"

"The poopers have jobs. They'll be far more committed to their non-human family. The four-legged lawnmowers arrive in a month or so. Maybe you need a big dumb puppy of your own. A golden retriever."

"Beth, if you're as good at picking out trees as you are at picking out poopers you'll be rich and famous by noon tomorrow."

CPA Chris called while we were on our way to buy trees. "Hey, good news! We just bought a supermarket on San Fernando."

"Why?" I asked.

"We need to create ten jobs for every immigrant visa and your girlfriend is an amazing salesperson. She's signed up 80 more people in Taipei since I left."

"How's she doing that?"

"Okay, talk to you soon!"

I knew Xyla was talented. I never knew how motivated working on commission would make her. I think we paid her 7% of $40 million that month? Who knows. All I know is her schedule was slammed for Indonesia and Chris was talking about building a skyscraper next to Magic Mountain.

Not long after I hung up with Chris, Martin called. "I'm not managing a fucking Vallejo," Martin said, out of the blue, one day, for some reason.

"Yes, you are," I said.

"I'll burn that fucking place down before I spend a single day there."

"Have you been there? Vallejo is the greatest supermarket around." And then I pulled out my ace distraction card. "Did you see Daniel Tiger on TV last night?"

"No. Why was he on TV?"

"I'll call you later."

BETH WAS HIGHLY ENTERTAINED by my conversations with Martin and Chris, judging by the crying, deafening laughter, and thick trails of black eyeliner smeared across her face. Which was hot. "Beth, this shit never ends. And it hasn't even started, yet. Do you know anyone who can manage a supermarket?"

"Carlito's ex-boyfriend used to run a not-so-super-market. Now he has a sausage place in Atwater Village."

"I think I know that guy. Syrian?"

"Yeah, Carlito showed me bukkake videos from the sausage guy's airplane hangar. That sausage guy can't get enough of my man's man chowder. He calls Carlito's cum his favorite chipotle aioli."

"Does that make you jealous?"

"Of course it does. I'm human. I love Carlito. Aren't you jealous Xyla is whoring herself out all over Asia selling cemetery investment derivatives?"

"I am now. I didn't know Xyla was doing that. Is sriracha the chipotle of Asia?"

BETH IN HER "GIVE ME A DISCOUNT" OUTFIT.

I didn't give a fuck. Beth didn't give a fuck as we pulled into the parking lot of the first tree farm, Beth braced me for impact. "Patrick, we're about to spend over a million dollars on trees."

In an unnecessarily creepy way, I said, "This is the greatest day of your life, isn't it, Beth?"

Beth's eyes watered a little bit as she said, "Let's fucking do this."

On the ground in tree town, Beth spoke to the assembled tree scientists in languages I never learned in community college. Mostly Latin. A lot like Beth's boy/girlfriend, Carlito Bandita, I imagine. As Beth lay on the ground next to some trees and leaned against others staring up into their canopies, she communicated with the immense creatures in ways I could never explain.

Wise far beyond her years, Beth never failed to astound. The solace her conviction and brutal honesty gave me when she said, "I'm in charge of these magnificent trees and all of the life they bring—the birds, the insects, the flora and fauna beneath their canopies—for the next 50 fucking years. At least. Fuck the fuck out of any motherfuck who fucking tries to fuck with my fucking shit around here as long as I fucking live," assured me we made the right decision when we hired Beth. Those words and, as importantly, her actions and verbal destruction of all motherfuckers in her way, convinced me to buy burial plots at The Last Resort for all who mattered to me. I wasn't just an employee, I was a customer. Thanks to Beth. Five stars.

"I've been here every week for years, Patrick," Beth said as we strolled beneath fantastic native Californians. "I know every tree. I know which ones are willing and able to come with me. I know their friends and family…" As her voice trailed off she recovered and said, "Patrick, if I don't fucking take these fuckers to Sylmar some cunt in San Clemente or Huntington fucking Beach will buy 'em and kill 'em all!"

"So, we're taking them all?"

"No!" Beth wailed. "Some of these fuckers want to live near the beach! There are still stupid motherfuckers who think Orange County is awesome."

"Trees? Fuck me. I thought trees were smarter than hillbillies."

I HAD NO IDEA BUYING TREES would be such an emotional rollercoaster. When did shopping for plants become a soul-shattering experience?

Beth sensed I was wrecked, so she twisted the knife in deeper. "What do you miss most about Xyla when she's gone?"

"I don't know, it's a long list. It's nice to have someone around who cares…"

"What about her lips?"

"Xyla has amazing lips. And that—"

"—tongue. I can only imagine that pretty little mouth of hers when—"

"WELCOME TO BURGER KING, MAY I TAKE YOUR ORDER!"

I told the two-way speaker box, "A Whopper and six orders of onion rings. Extra crispy."

Beth may not have known how much fun she could have with onion rings and an erect penis before our road head—er, road trip. God bless America, and, from the bottom of my box of onion rings, thank you, Burger King.

"WHY AREN'T YOU RUNNING THE WHOLE DEAL?" Beth asked as we neared Sylmar.

"I'm too melancholy."

"Too melancholy? Too melancholy to run a cemetery? That's impossible."

I wanted to choke Beth. Again. She still had some Burger King onion ring residue glued to her lower lip. Which was hot. "You're stupid, Beth. Go home to your girl/boyfriend and show they what you learned today."

"Fuck you, Patrick. I quit."

"Great. I'll find someone else to watch grass grow."

I SAID, "HAVE IT YOUR WAY." SHE DID.

I DIDN'T WANT TO FACE THE DAY, BUT I DID. Hungover, fried, and covered in fried breadcrumbs, I called a friend. "Chris, I'm afraid we'll need to find a new landscape director."

"I know, Beth's in the hospital. They had to pump her stomach."

"Again? It's not soccer season. What was it? The onion rings?"

"Yeah, a couple of dozen onion rings and a gerbil wrapped in duct tape."

"Oh. So that's why she was in that truck stop so long."

"Beth passed out and drove her Cybertruck through the quincieñera dress shop on Foothill."

"Which one?"

"The one the taco truck always parks in front of."

"Which one? There's a dozen of those."

"The one next to the piñata store."

"That narrows it down," I said, sarcastically. "Which one of those?"

"Siempre Quince."

"Forever 15?"

"Always 15. Go to the hospital right now, bring Beth flowers, she's a superstar. We are fucked without her."

"Tell me about it. I'll bring onion rings, too."

7
BUILD IT, THEY WILL DIE

BETH RECOVERED FROM HER ONION RING/GERBIL INCIDENT and returned to the construction site with renewed vigor. We demolished four baseball diamonds, constructed the greenhouse, built a vineyard and hops trellises, planted the food forest, and added chickens, a goose, and a donkey to the family. The trees we bought in San Diego arrived and the beautiful, gnarled, mature olives, oaks, sycamores, willows, and other cool super-expensive monsters went straight into the ground guarded by steel bulldozer traps to prevent the construction workers from murdering mother nature. As the construction process allowed, shrubs, flowers, giant bamboo, and more trees went into the ground.

Sylmar had been such an ugly hellhole before. We couldn't stop beautifying the place with foliage. Beth built dams and weirs and dug swales and trenches in and around the wash next to the baseball bullshit where torrential floods tore through the neighborhood with every rainstorm. We were able to capture all of the water we needed to feed every living thing on the property and bank hundreds of thousands of gallons just in case.

The golf course transformation into a luxury resort/entertainment destination remained on target due to the outstanding performance of starchitect Golden Richards and the team of overqualified contractors we hired. As the resort morphed from fantasy to reality Martin started to freak out. "There's no way I can manage a cemetery, a resort, and a supermarket at the same time."

"Let's go to Las Vegas," I said.

Martin looked at me like I was crazy. and asked, "How are hookers going to solve my problems?"

I stared at Martin long enough for him to figure out how stupid he was. Then I said, "We're going to Las Vegas Friday to find someone to do all that shit."

Out of the blue, Martin's wife, Martina, showed up and asked me, "How's your sex life, Patrick?"

"I need more oral and a vagina once in a while wouldn't hurt. Why do you ask? Are you offering a quick hand—"

"Wow, I feel like I should be offended rather than aroused. Most people don't respond in such graphic detail—"

"Sorry. I should have pretended I don't want you to swallow my cock. Martina, you must realize, every person with a cock wants to shove their dick down your throat. Spit in my hand"

"Yes, I know that. Grab my hair. Forty percent of the people I blow want me to swallow it, 30% want me to let it spill out of my mouth onto my tits, and the rest are too shy to ask me to spit it back in their mouth or want super sick shit, like dog bowl shit. It's just a load of cum, I've dealt with a million of those. Tell me what you want. Don't be shy."

"Have you ever been to Krispy Kreme?"

Martina knew I needed the love of my life, Xyla, by my side. So I begged Xyla to return from Indonesia to our grave-adjacent home in Sylmar.

"Xyla, please come back. It's so dead around here. I can't live without you. Slow jams just don't sound the same."

"Stop crying. Slow jams don't sound the same here, either, Patrick. Karaoke is painful."

"I'm going crazy from the heat."

"That's a David Lee Roth book."

"You know I love you."

"You love every young, hot, slutty, Asian, goth supermodel who shoves your cock down her even hotter Colombian sorority sister's throat."

"I find that disgusting."

"No, you didn't."

"You broke my heart, Xyla."

"You broke my hymen, Patrick."

THE LAST RESORT'S ORGANIZATIONAL CULTURE DICTATED a Friday lunch/happy hour celebration every week which boosted morale and fomented teamwork amongst the entire crazy collection of wackos we'd assembled. We invited every employee of ours, the entire construction crew, and random people from the community to participate in the festivities. Martin's crew at The 19th Hole barbecued. Beth organized the beer pong games. A good time was always had by all.

On this particular Friday I spotted an outlier across the room talking to Golden Richards. A spectacular vision of beauty floating within an aura of awesomeness. I observed the beguiling creature for twenty seconds and deduced exactly what she would smell and taste like.

I approached the fantastic woman and my golden wingman introduced us, "Ava, this is Patrick."

I glued my gaze into Ava's emerald eyes and said, "You only have one chance, Ava."

"To make a first impression," the mind-reading woman responded.

"We're leaving for Las Vegas in an hour."

"Yes. We are."

My approach to dating is: set the appointment; shut the fuck up. Anything I say after the appointment is set will not help, it will only hurt. I found Beth and put her in charge of making sure Ava was prepared to travel to Vegas on our party bus and hang out for a couple of days and nights. Daniel Tiger had graciously invited us to crash at his Las Vegas penthouse, what could go wrong?

Whilst Beth concierged my new girlfriend, Ava Avalon, into submission, a person walked into The 19th Hole. Instinctively, I knew they were Carlito Bandita. And I knew they would fuck my whole deal with Ava up if they interrupted Beth.

"You're Carlito."

"Yes, I am."

"Follow me. We have a drink named after you."

"You have a drink named Dave?"

With that classic retort, I knew Carlito was a legend. "You've hit the jackpot with Beth, Carlito. She is one in a million."

"She's not very nice to me. She treats me like shit and beats me every time she comes home from work if she's had to interact with you."

"You must like it or you wouldn't stick around."

"Yeah…"

"You're welcome."

I ordered two Carlito Banditas from Martin's bartender-in-training, and within moments we were drinking margaritas. "Carlito, what do you do when you're not hanging out with us here for happy hour?"

"I knit, I play guitar in a band with El Jefe from NOFX, and sometimes I read," Carlito explained. "I don't need to work."

Because Carlito looked a little bit brain-damaged I asked they, "Are you a disabled vet?"

"No, I invented that little stick thing Starbucks puts in the hole of the coffee lid. Checks show up in my mailbox every 90 days, so I'm good."

"No fucking way."

"Way."

"What the hell are those stick things in the coffee cups called?"

"Splash sticks."

"Do you like fish sticks?"

"What?"

"Do you like fish sticks?"

"Of course, I love fish sticks."

Beth showed up and said, "Really? The fish dicks joke, Patrick? Ava's down for whatever, I told her you'll take her shopping in Vegas."

SUPERSTAR AVA AVALON. THERE ARE NO WORDS...

"Beth, you are employee of the month. And your Carlito is something else. This weekend will be the greatest."

"Weekend? It's spring break next week. You and Ava won't be back for a while. Try not to fuck this one up, Patrick. Ava is a goddess. I know more about her after a 15-minute conversation than you'll know about her in 15 years. You'll never meet another woman like Ava."

"Yeah, Patrick," Carlito Bandita said, "try not to fuck this one up."

ON THE PARTY BUS TO LAS VEGAS, I kept my distance from Ava, admiring her radiant glamour from afar. Until I couldn't anymore because she sat down next to me and said, "Beth says her poquita Bandita has beautiful boobs."

"I hope she didn't tell you anything about me."

"I know everything about you. I've been watching you."

"With binoculars?"

"A telescope."

"That's not at all creepy, officer. What's your deal, Ava?"

"I run the human resources department at the community college."

"You're hired. We need an HR person."

"I don't want to work with you, Patrick. I want a romance with you."

"Aren't we supposed to pretend we don't like each other that much for a while?"

"We can do that later."

Martin appeared and rudely interrupted the staring contest Ava was winning. "Daniel Tiger had to fly to New York for some kind of hair frizz emergency with Mariah. He won't be around but we're still staying at his place."

"Great, less distraction action. Ava is going to help us find our food and beverage director. She's also in charge of finding us a human resources or whatever person."

"No, I'm not," Ava said. "Do you know how hard it is to find someone willing to move from Las Vegas to Sylmar?"

"Did you just ask me if I know how hard it is?"

Beth glared at me from across the aisle of the bus. "Don't be creepy, Patrick." That's when I got up and told the bus driver to pull over at the next truck stop where I bought a roll of duct tape. The sound of duct tape being ripped from the roll sent visible shivers down Beth's spine. Ava and I were thoroughly amused.

"When do we get to see Carlito's DDs?" Ava asked.

"I brought mushrooms."

"I want mushrooms."

"They're in my pocket."

Somewhere around Barstow Ava retrieved a Ziploc bag from my pocket using nothing but her mouth, lips, teeth, and tongue as her chin aggressively dug into my genitals. I couldn't have been more impressed. By the time we crossed the border into Nevada, Ava and I were on another planet.

"Tell me something about Ava."

"I'm a cellist."

"So, you're into Bach and Yo-Yo Ma?"

"Sure, I play Bach. Everybody knows Bach. My favorite composer is Xenakis."

"Xenakis? What planet are you from, Ava?"

"You'll find out."

"Have you been to Greece?"

"I'm dying to go."

"Me, too. Do you have your passport with you?"

"Of course."

I checked flights on my phone and told Ava, "We're leaving for Athens tomorrow afternoon at 4 p.m. We'll be in Greece at 4 p.m. Sunday. There's only one thing you need to do."

A CONFUSED BLACK PATRICK. BEFORE THE MUSHROOMS, AFTER THE DUCT TAPE.

"Only one?"

"Only one. One a day. Before we leave for Greece, you need to help me find a food and beverage director in Las Vegas."

BY BRUNCH TIME THE NEXT MORNING finding a food and beverage director was the last thing on my mind—Ava and I were planning all things Greek. Until I saw an old British friend walk by. "Nik!"

"Paddy! What are you doing here?"

"Tripping balls. I thought you were in Hawaii."

"That resort burned down. I'm doing food and beverage shit here now."

"No, you're not. Do you want to move back to LA?"

"Yes. I hate Las Vegas."

"How much money do you need to make to run a 120-room resort in Los Angeles?"

"£150,000 annually plus benefits. Real benefits, not shitty American benefits."

"How many weeks of vacation do you need?" I asked.

"Six weeks," Nik said.

"If you get six weeks everybody gets six weeks. Can we afford that, Ava?"

"Yes," Ava replied.

No wonder I liked asking Ava yes or no questions. Ava, Nik, and I took the elevator to Daniel Tiger's place and introduced The Last Resort posse to Nik, the crew demanded Nik join our fiesta, I Venmo'd Nik his first six months' pay, and then Ava and I left for the airport. Mission fucking accomplished.

"**A**VA, ARE YOU A MAGNET FOR ALL things awesome?" I asked the new object of all of my emotions. "I hadn't seen Nik or even talked to the guy in seven or eight years. He appeared out of nowhere at the exact time we needed each other."

"No."

Nik. He thinks we don't see him. "Hi, Nik!"

"Great, thanks for the honest answer."

Ava left me hanging for a few, then said, "I have selective magnetism."

"What does that mean?"

"I can control my magnetism. I focus it and direct it when needed to get what I want."

"Do you have one or more of the disorders in that big book about crazy people?"

"*The Diagnostic and Statistical Manual of Mental Disorders?*" Ava asked.

"Yeah, that's the one."

"Sure, everybody does. That book is a thousand pages of problems, big and small, endemic to human existence. We all have serious issues, it's whether or not we use them for evil or not that distinguishes people."

"So, what you're saying is, everybody is capable of extreme evil?"

"Do I have to say it?"

"Yes."

"It."

As soon as Ava fell asleep I texted CPA Chris:

> *I hired the world's greatest*
> *food and beverage guy*
> *Nik will be in Sylmar Friday*
> *I'm on a plane to Greece*
> *Will be in touch when I get back*
> *In case of emergency dial 911*

Greece? The country?

> *Yes, that Greece. I met the HR person from the college and decided to take her to Greece.*

Ha! Ava finally made her move!

What the fuck is going on around here? What the fuck does that mean? Where the fuck is the flight attendant? I need whiskey!

8
GREECE/MALTA

A WISE MAN ONCE SAID, "All of the best French fries are made in Greece." Or maybe he said grease. Anyway, about Giannis Klearchou Xenakis. War hero, composer, architect, author, mathematician—the definition of a champion in action. Sentenced to death by a right-wing regime similar to one the stupid motherfuckers in Alabama who elect "college" football coaches to political office dream about. Xenakis was a dude designed in some kind of eugenics laboratory to make the rest of us feel like losers. That's one reason Ava and I embarked upon our Xenakis-themed impromptu excursion to Greece.

As our airplane descended into Athens and the anti-anxiety medications lost their luster, I told Ava, "We're not leaving Greece until I buy a bouzouki."

"I know a guy," Ava responded.

We landed in Athens, got hammered in the hotel bar, and contemplated staying in that hotel forever.

"The hookers are so hot here. And so inexpensive," Ava said. "This is the greatest hotel bar ever!" I couldn't argue with her observations. Whatever happened to the Grecian economy that made Athenian prostitutes less expensive than Vietnamese whores had more to do with trickle-down economics than Ava could trickle down in a lifetime. I don't complain in the face of the face of ecstatic adversity. Can you blame me?

After a couple of days of Parthenons and Vaginathons in Athens, Ava and I hit the road to experience Greece through the eyes of our hero, Xenakis.

Day three in Greece included a day trip to Corinth and a visit to an especially significant locale in the legend of Xenakis—Mycenae. My understanding of the Xenakis connection to Mycenae is, he brought a bunch of musicians, psychedelic light shows, a giant ahead-of-its-time synthesizer, and some farm animals to ruins of structures built by Cyclopes and partied in 1978 like it was 1999. That's my version of the story and I'm sticking to it.

Because Xenakis fought the evil British imperialists for an independent Greece in his college days, the right-wing wackos in the junta fat bastard Winston Churchill installed, (FBC = Fat Bastard Churchill) who stole Greece from the Greeks, sentenced Xenakis to death in absentia. Xenakis saw this bullshit coming and got the fuck out of there, ending up in a place called Paris, France.

"Churchill loved nothing more than brick-laying," I told my newish friend Ava.

"True. You know what brick-laying means, right?" Ava asked.

An amused man, myth, and legend, Giannis Xenakis. Before he died, after the British blew his face apart with an artillery shell.

"Of course I do. It means taking a bunch of bricks, some mortar—"

"Winston Churchill's favorite thing to do was to get plowed in the ass by big black cocks."

"Plural?"

"And then some."

I thought about what Ava said, questioned all of the historical bullshit I believed to be fact, and asked Ava, "So, when Benjamin Franklin said he was flying a kite…"

A call from Daniel Tiger interrupted our historical conversation. The nosy little fat bastard asked, "Where are you, Black Patrick?"

"We're on a ferry in the Sardonic Gulf, headed to Naxos," I answered. "Then we're off to Crete."

"Hi, Daniel Tiger!" Ava said.

"Jesus fucking Christ. Crete? Crete sucks," Daniel Tiger opined. "And it's the Saronic Gulf, you moron. Go look at a statue or something, then find your way back to Athens and fly to Malta. You're staying at my place in Valletta."

"Is Greece the European version of the Philippines?" I asked the cranky fucker who interrupted my vacation for no reason.

"Are you sniffing glue or gasoline, Patrick?" Daniel asked, in a huff.

"Yes. What's so great about Malta?" I asked Mr. Tiger.

"You'll see. Tell me when your flight arrives and I'll meet you at the airport," and then Daniel ended the call.

The slightly tipsy and endlessly charming Ava asked, "Is Daniel the Maltese Tiger?"

"I don't know what the fuck Daniel Tiger is."

Based solely on the strength of Daniel Tiger's hair products, Ava insisted we eschew Crete and redirect to Malta, so we did. We didn't tell Daniel Tiger when we were arriving on Malta, we intended to spend a day or so exploring on our own, however, somehow, the bastard figured some shit out and awaited our arrival at L-Ajruport Internazzjonali ta'

Malta. Daniel Tiger's place in Valletta turned out to be a palatial building on St. George's Square with cafes, bars, and restaurants on the ground floor, and massive apartments on the upper floor. Ava claimed she pushed the wrong button in the elevator and found a portal to another dimension, but I attributed that to psilocybin mushroom flashbacks.

"Ava, what do you wanna be when you grow up?"

"I don't know. I want to start painting again."

"Art?"

"No. People, silly. Paintings. People painting. That reminds me. We forgot to see Carlito's boobs."

The last thing I wanted to see was Carlito Bandita's boobs, but I said, "Fuck!" anyway. The mental image was damaging enough.

"Are you a goth?"

"No. I'm a Visigoth."

"We can stay here forever if we want to," I told Ava. "You've never looked so beautiful to me anywhere else."

"We met seven days ago," Ava accurately commented. "We've been seven or eight places together. Two of those were Starbucks."

"I know, but who's counting? Is this whirlwind of a spring break romance all we will ever have?"

"Probably. That's the way the ball bounces, sometimes. And, if this is all we get, that's okay."

"I don't think I like your fuckin' attitude, Ava."

"Thank you, Dr. Phil."

"We'll be right back."

THE SPECTACULAR WEATHER, MAGNIFICENT ARCHITECTURE, inside jokes, and occasional, random Daniel Tiger appearances made the ten days I spent with Ava on Malta the greatest ten days of my life. Until we ran out of shit to talk about. "I know now Xenakis is your favorite composer. Do you have a favorite rock band?"

"The Who."

"Wow."

"Why do you say 'wow'?" Ava asked.

"Nobody ever says that. It's always the Beatles, or the Stones, or Sabbath—"

"Those people have never listened to *Quadrophenia* on acid."

At that point, I blacked out. Speechless. *Who is this relentlessly awesome creature from another planet?* I asked my comatose self. *Is she going to tell me she plays a Firebird bass through an Ampeg SVT next?*

I told Ava, "One time, in London, I woke up in a Soho doorway, a policeman knew my name."

Ava asked me, "Who the fuck are you?"

"I am Black Patrick."

"Why are you so weird?" Ava asked.

"On the seventh hour of the seventh day of the seventh month, the seventh doctor said I'm the hoochie-coochie man. Gypsy woman told my mama pretty much the same thing. It's a lot of stress. Sorry if I'm a little tense."

Ava couldn't put on her headset fast enough. I knew our time together in Europe could never be repeated in California or anywhere else. Whatever. Fuck this planet. Ava knew the same thing.

As our plane descended into LAX I asked Ava, "Is this some kind of *Lost in Translation* thing?"

"Yes," Ava answered, "I think so."

"So, I'm Bill Murray and you're Reese Witherspoon?"

Ava wanted to kill me. She should have. "You motherfucker—" She knew I knew it was Scarlett, not Reese, but Ava still wanted to kill me.

"*Lost in Translation* is my favorite movie, Ava."

Ava appeared stunned, shocked, and stopped in her tracks. Like the most beautiful deer in headlights with high beams I had ever seen. A tear formed in the corner of her left eye and, for the first time, Ava said, "I love you, Patrick."

9
BACH IN SYLMAR

"How's the cemetery business, Black Patrick?" a man known as Daniel Tiger asked.

"I don't fucking know. I just got back from Malta. Thanks, again. I'm busy trying to figure out who accidentally sent me an order of ramen for lunch today. Best fucking ramen I've ever had, by far."

An enraged Daniel Tiger screamed, "You ate my fucking ramen!"

"That was your ramen? That shit was delicious. It's not my fault you don't know how to use GrubHub."

When Ava and I returned to the United States of America, we parted ways. I presumed it was a permanent goodbye. A big crate from Greece was waiting for me in Sylmar. A few cases of wine, more olive oil than Nik could ever drizzle over whatever he drizzled it over, a bouzouki, and a zither. I didn't remember buying a zither, but that's the way the ball bounces. I sent the zither to Ava's office with the UPS guy and forgot about it and her. The end, what a great story.

At The Last Resort, much had changed. For the better. Work on the entire crazy facility screamed ahead of schedule and Liquid Death Amphitheater at The Last Resort was finished months in advance of its due date. Because that's the way Lemmy would have done it. So, with the stage set for rock 'n' roll, keyboard genius Tiko and I put the band back together with Daniel Tiger on drums and Royce on bass. We ran the sound system, the lighting rig, and the neighbors through the ultimate test. No more than five minutes after our show commenced with, "We are Xenakis. We play rock 'n' roll," local dogs and residents began to howl. I swear I saw birds fall from the sky. Recent Sylmar transplant, Nik, rode his electric bicycle around the neighborhood gauging community reaction to the largest, most deadly, sound system in Sylmar history.

"The bass was loud as fuck at the hospital," Nik reported.

"That's not good," I remarked. "Olive View is two miles away and the amphitheater is pointed in the opposite direction."

"My professional opinion: fuck 'em," Nik stated over the wail of car alarms set off by the subwoofers we buried in grave holes all over the property. "Fuck 'em."

Part of me wondered if the prudent move would be to cancel the first annual Liquid Death Sylmar Death Metal

Fiesta set to inaugurate our facility in a few weeks. The other part of me said, "Fuck 'em."

Word spread around the graveyard Tiko had some issues. Major issues.

So I asked him the obvious question, "Tiko, are you using drugs?"

"Every day."

"Good, that's not the problem. What's wrong?"

"The Chinese. We already have at least a hundred relocation sales booked. I am fucked. Do you know how long it takes to dig up a body?"

"No, but that's a great business plan. You need to hire some help. Do we need to go visit some cemeteries in Las Vegas?"

"That might help. My big concern is, I can't hire people to help me dig up those graves in East LA. I need to do it myself. There's a lot of shit buried down there nobody was ever supposed to see, remember?"

"Oh, yeah. I forgot about that. If Xyla ever comes back from Asia or wherever she is we can put her in charge of the Chinese division."

"She's not coming back."

"What makes you say that?" I asked Tiko.

"Xyla has a sugar daddy in Malaysia, a sugar daddy in Jakarta, a sugar daddy—"

"Fuck you, Tiko. Maybe we need to go scout for some body-planting talent in Macao. They say Macao is like a New Orleans/Las Vegas combo town."

"With yakuza."

"Wrong country. I'm going to Macao. Are you in?"

"No, have fun. I'm not leaving East LA for the next few years."

"MARTIN, WE'RE FUCKED."

"What else is new?"

"Tiko's out. He doesn't want to leave East LA. We need someone new to run the body-burying operation."

"I know exactly what we do," Martin said. "We set up a job fair at the First Annual Liquid Death Amphitheater Sylmar Death Metal Fiesta at The Last Resort."

"Dude, Tiko was a huge part of our whole business plan. We don't know shit about dealing with dead bodies. We're fucked."

"Let's hire one of those drug cartel guys who dissolve bodies in barrels of acid."

"That's not a bad idea. Flights are dirt cheap to Colombia right now."

"Really?"

"No. We need to go visit every funeral home around here and steal some dead people people. I know we'll find some motivated and enthusiastic assistant funeral home manager dying, no pun intended, for the opportunity to run a people-planting operation of his or her own. Like a champion. We'll know 'em when we see 'em."

Slow-moving man Martin said, "Sure, let's plan on that."

"No, motherfucker. Right now. We can't fuck this part of our business up, it'll be $15 to 20 million in revenue a year, minimum."

I WISH I COULD SAY OUR LAP around the San Fernando Valley meeting funeral people wasn't the most depressing way to spend a day. What a drag. Thank God The 19th Hole was overstocked with tequila. Post funeral home excursion and well into double-digit double-shot territory a guy called and said, "Hey, I'm Royce from Dignity Death, my manager said you're looking for a funeral director."

"Yes, we are. Get over here."

OVERQUALIFIED UNDERTAKER, ROYCE. A CHAMPION IN ACTION.

Royce arrived in twenty minutes. He looked like a junkie and a dude on a spectrum or two. Pale, almost translucent skin, massive black circles under his eyes, and dressed like Johnny

Cash. In other words, after he said, "I need tequila," we knew he was perfect. We reviewed Royce's resume and asked him if he knew what to do with a dead body, he told us he knew everything about dead people, had a degree in mortuary science, four years of experience in funeral sales, embalming, cremating, and funeral directing. We learned we needed to build a dead body building with a people/pizza oven instead of a ghost kitchen, but we all agreed to call it The Ghost Kitchen, anyway. And Royce demanded a hearse.

New rule at The Last Resort—all prospective employees had to pass the Friday Happy Hours test and be unanimously approved by Martin, Beth, Nik, and myself. Royce made the cut, poor bastard.

"Nik, who can run the hotel?"

"Not fucking me. I know someone."

"Can you get them here now? And you need someone to run Rainbow Bar & Grill."

CPA Chris showed up unexpectedly at our Friday Happy Hours blowout. "You need to start hiring a lot of people or we may have to return some of the immigration visa investment money."

"Fuck!" Martin and I screamed in unison.

Overnight Beth had a dozen new cultivators propagating flora and landscapers making The Last Resort beautiful, Martin's operations staff ballooned with new maintenance, security, and administrative personnel, Nik had a crew of cooks and servers training, Royce figured out the cremation oven burned hot enough to cast iron, bronze, and fire porcelain, so he hired a couple of artistic types to craft urns and decorative ornaments.

THE COMPANY CAR.

"THE BRAVER THE PROGRAMMING, the better the audience," I told Martin when he asked what I had planned for the Liquid Death Amphitheater at The Last Resort. "Everything we ever do here needs to be weird as fuck. The entire premise is weird as fuck, the music might as well be."

"Speak for yourself."

"For the entire first year, all we do is weird-ass classical music. I canceled the death metal festival. We do kick-ass contemporary classical shit from Eastern Europe, weirdos from CalArts, all of the greatest fingernails-on-a-chalkboard shit."

"Why?"

"The neighbors won't complain. They can't. We're a scrappy little classical music venue. You can't complain about classical music."

"If you say so."

"The second year we bring on the punk bands. The death metal. King Diamond Week will be an annual thing. For the children."

"Where's Ava?" Martin asked, in an attempt to derail our conversation.

"I don't know. She's around."

"I saw her walking into the college with her cello the other day."

"Cool."

"Put her in charge of the music programming."

"Done. I need to fill the calendar in the nightclub, too, and we need jazz bands for the speakeasy."

Martin added, "And we need DJs for the douchebag rooftop deck, too."

"Fuck. Do you know Harvey?" I asked Martin.

"Who's Harvey?"

"Hang Glider Harvey. Everybody knows Harvey. Let's go say hello to Hang Glider Harvey."

FROM THE TOP OF THE MOUNTAIN overlooking our cemetery resort in progress, I sent a text to Ava and told her, "I'm flying into your arms. Look at the sky in 10 minutes." I have no idea what the emojis she responded with meant.

"I'm not jumping off the top of this mountain with this helmet and a kite," Martin said.

"No shit, Martin. You're *running* off the top of this mountain. Here, snort some of this." And off he went. Sylmar is known as the world capital of hang gliding. From the mountain-top launch site to the landing zone the distance measured about two miles as the Martin flies. It was slightly windy and I wasn't sure where Martin went, but that didn't stop me.

MARTIN NEVER HAD A GOOD IDEA or knew how to live like Monty Python—he never looked on the bright side of life. "Golden Richards says the cemetery sales store is way too big. He believes it will look like a giant, empty real estate office if we give it 6,000 square feet. I can't think of anything that makes sense to put in there alongside our dead people business and the flower shop."

"I can. Fine art. Really expensive works of museum-quality art."

"How much revenue will we see from a couple of thousand square feet of art?"

"Who cares? It doesn't matter if we ever sell anything. We need a place to stash all of the Chinese cash. Would you rather hang $10 million worth of art in a storefront open 12 hours a week or add another grocery store to your portfolio of painful businesses?"

"I think we should open an art gallery!"

"Great idea, Martin! You're on fire today," I told the uncharacteristically upbeat Martin. "Here's the deal. We never, ever, no matter what, discuss the art business or the art gallery. No emails, no phone calls, nothing. The art business is full of every kind of crime humans have ever invented, so much so the FBI has a special division devoted exclusively to art fraud."

"Why would we want to invite unnecessary scrutiny by entering the art space, then?"

"I think it'll be fun. Seriously, a legit fine art gallery gives us luxury cred and an excuse to invite the Sylmar cognoscenti to an upscale shindig every month or so."

Martin shook his head, mumbled something about "Sylmar cognoscenti," retreated to his office in The 19th Hole, and calculated the odds of a fatality in an intentional hang-gliding accident. I started looking at flights and hotels for my upcoming trip to Art Basel in Miami Beach.

MARTIN LIKED TO BE A BIG DOWNER, SOMETIMES. "You know about the tunnel disaster, right?"

Here we go again. "Yeah. It's a bullshit story."

"What makes you think that?"

"Do you really believe defense contractor Lockheed was down there boring a water tunnel 200 feet underground? A couple of months after a huge earthquake leveled the entire neighborhood? The day after a methane leak was detected and every inspector ordered them to stop digging. Insane."

"You think they were building an interdimensional gateway to the lizard people?"

"No. Not to the lizard people. *FOR* the lizard people. We work for them. We're slaves to your heroes, and all of them are lizard people. Musk, Bezos, Jobs, Hagar, Fieri—"

"Nik is a huge fan of Triple-D."

"We're fucked! I quit."

"I saw Ava wheeling her cello out of the parking garage yesterday. You should call her."

"Martin, you should shut the fuck up and mind your own Vallejo."

I HATE PHONES, so I went next door to the community college and knocked on Ava's office door.

"Wow, you have a lot of soundproofing going on in here."

"I had to add that. For the cello. Every time I practice Penderecki people think I'm getting raped in here."

"I shall not accept your invitation to violate you, you minx."

"Ligeti?"

I don't remember much about what happened after that. The noises Ava made with such a large instrument between her legs made me want to crawl up into some kind of cello birth canal.

"Why are we strangers?" Ava asked.

Well, when in doubt, I tend to quote a man named Ian Gillan. "We must remain perfect strangers."

"Ritchie Blackmore wants me to join his creepy faux-medieval band."

"He wants a cellist?"

"No. He says I'm the most beautiful shawmer."

"I'm sure you are. What's a shawmer?"

"Someone who plays a shawm. It's a big, loud woodwind, similar to an oboe. I keep telling Ritchie to stop calling me. He's a married man."

"I don't trust people who wear those pilgrim hats."

"Ritchie likes to see me with things in my mouth."

"Here's my idea, Ava. Blackmore's Night, a month-long residency at Liquid Death Amphitheater at The Last Resort to inaugurate our new venue. We're building an identical reproduction of Rainbow Bar & Grill, the stars are aligned. Call Ritchie right now."

Ava called Ritchie, he gave Ava a crazy number to perform at The Last Resort for a month, Ava gave Ritchie a crazy number back to play shawm in his band, and then I called a man named Tiger. Daniel Tiger.

"When's my room ready, motherfucker?" Daniel asked.

"Six weeks, Daniel, eight weeks. Send me $5 million right now."

"Why?"

"Because that's what Ritchie fucking Blackmore told me to tell you to do." And then I ended the call. A few minutes later I had $5 million for a few minutes. Then, about 30 seconds after that, Blackmore's Night had $4.8 million, and, to top it all off, their new shawmer received the remaining $200,000.

In obvious shock, Ava started at her phone and said, "You just made me the highest-paid shawmer in history."

"I did nothing, Ritchie recognizes your talent. Please remember me when you're gone and I'm stuck in Sylmar fucking California with Ritchie's wife and her hurdy-gurdy collection."

"There are worse people you can be stuck with," Ava said. "I've seen Candice do things with velcro, latex, and the business end of a cricket bat even I couldn't imagine."

"Which end of a cricket bat is the business end? The sticky wicket?"

"I'll let Candice show you. For your birthday."

Before I knew it, Ava was gone, probably forever, rehearsing bagpipe music with Ritchie Blackmore and a bunch of white people prancing in a forest somewhere.

Daniel Tiger didn't look happy. "They hate us, 'cause they ain't us."

"What? This is the first time we've ever done anything and people don't hate us. Yet. Try not to fuck it up."

"Black Patrick, you're a stupid motherfucker. How do you think I made my first billion?"

"Selling shampoo on QVC to fat people poppin' pills in the Midwest watching television. You're able to convince obese women all they need to be happy is some chocolate cake-smelling shit in their greasy heads of patchy hair."

"Those fat fuck trailer park people hate us. Because they ain't us. But they still buy our deep-penetrating maple syrup conditioner."

"Us? Our? I'm not part of your goddamned hair product company."

"You're right. Hair products are not your deal. The Black Patrick Facial Formula. That's you."

"Daniel, are you smoking crack, again?"

"Yeah, sometimes. It takes the edge off the speed."

"You're doing it all wrong! Xanax takes the edge off the speed. You're still on fire because of the amphetamines, but the Xanax makes sure you don't act like a wife-beating cop from Florida."

Daniel said, "I know you hate cops, and I do too, but I hate seeing cops get killed."

"I actually agree, to some extent. Deportation to Argentina works for me."

"When a cop gets killed, every pig in the state shows up and they have a little parade from the hospital to some other place. If fire trucks are around they spray water from the fucking fire trucks over the arriving hearse, for some reason. Maybe because the hearse smells like a dead pig. Like somebody's makin' bacon."

"Daniel Tiger, you just gave me goosebumps."

"Do you bury cops here?"

"Fuck no. We only bury ethical people here. Not cunts who cram a bunch of bogus overtime into their last year on the job so their pension payments are fraudulently inflated the rest of their lives."

"Good answer. Fuck the police. Speaking of Xanax, I hear Xyla's back in town."

"Who cares?"

"Me. She's hanging out with Royce and she knows you have a new girlfriend. She wants to work with Beth growing flowers and whatever. So I hired her."

"Thanks, Daniel, I think."

"Be nice to her. You're going to need her."

10
FINISH LINE

THE LAST 10% OF ANYTHING IS THE MOST DIFFICULT, people who never finish anything say. The Last Resort ramped up the whole goddamned operation to power through—crush, if you will—the final detail work needed to make our resort the greatest five-star cemetery resort in the San Fernando Valley from Day One.

"Golden, what's left?" I asked our starchitectural superhero.

"We're good. The electrical inspection passed, and we're all set for final next week. Stained glass going in chapel today. All good."

"Martin, any issues?"

"All good in the resort. A few more pieces of furniture and artwork and we're ready to rock."

"Nik?"

"The Rainbow is staffed, the Wine Catacomb, too. The nightclub is good to go. I'm still interviewing bikini servers for the rooftop. Wine cellar stocked, booze stocked, freezers full, perishables on order."

"Beth?"

"Ready now. We have plenty of merchandise for the Outdoor Market."

"Royce?"

"We need dead bodies. Other than that, everything is perfect."

"Brilliant. Invited guests start arriving in 14 days for the soft opening. We'll have a full house. Mostly journalists, celebrities, influencers, and other losers. Be nice to 'em anyway. The grand opening is in four weeks. Blackmore's Night starts their residency in about five weeks."

"Oh, I forgot to tell you," Martin said. "CPA Chris disappeared with all of our money."

"Aw, fuck," I dejectedly screamed. "We need to open tomorrow, then."

"SO, WHERE DID ALL THE MONEY GO, BLACK PATRICK?"

"What money?" I asked Daniel Tiger.

"The money your mother gave you for singing lessons. That was the worst karaoke version of *Close to You* the planet has ever heard."

"We're totally fucked. We're so fucked we had to start a karaoke night. I'd ask you to invest more cash in our doomed enterprise but it'll be more fun to watch the Chinese Communist Party cunts murder us all."

"Patrick, you're a total asshole, but you've always treated me with the appropriate level of disdain."

"Thanks, Daniel. I think."

"I had Taylor's roadies deliver a road case to your office earlier."

"Philthy Animal?"

"Whatever. Here's the key. Don't tell Martin. Or Beth. You can only trust Ava, Nik, Royce, and Xyla around here. Everybody else will stab you in the back."

"Cool, thanks."

Punch-drunk and dumbstruck by the gut punch Chris delivered to our burgeoning enterprise, I sat in silence wondering how our crazy plan had reached this phase in its disintegration so quickly. Until Royce ran into the Rainbow and said, "Motherfucker, let's go!"

Royce had chained a giant road case to the back of a golf cart and we roared off towards the caretaker's house where he and Xyla made happiness together. "What are we gonna do with all of this shit?" Royce asked. I assumed the road case was filled with Daniel Tiger pomade or something like that.

"What the fuck do people usually do with shampoo?" I asked Royce.

"Dude, the road case is full of cash! $100 bills!"

I turned around and looked behind the golf cart at the giant road case big enough to fit Mick Jagger's scarf collection and screamed, "Slow the fuck down!" as we passed one of Beth's deep, dark ponds, suddenly in fear of a rollover golf cart accident.

Why did Daniel Tiger leave Martin and Beth out of the trustworthy gang? There was no rhyme or reason to his list of people he deemed trustworthy. Sure, Xyla didn't care about money—she pocketed almost $20 million acquiring our immigration investment visa cash and was smart enough to stash her funds without the help of our crooked accountant. And Xyla was only around because Royce was around, and vice versa. Their lives were not motivated by greed.

Nik, much like generations of cool punk rock people from the United fucking Kingdom, detested rich people. And, the love of my life, Ava, spurned the advances of temporarily-wealthy film and television cunts in Los Angeles ritually. When she wasn't "rehearsing" that leprechaun music with Ritchie Blackmore.

Daniel Tiger's lifeline would only last so long. Too bad we didn't have a fucking accountant around to help us figure out exactly how long. Thank God so many of our guests used cash to purchase thousands and thousands of concert tickets in the amphitheater every week, allegedly, so we could deposit insane amounts of cash into the bank.

Daniel Tiger always seemed to drop into the Rainbow at the most unexpected of times.

"I see your concert ticket business is starting to lift off, Black Patrick. How are your finances?"

"We're fucked," I told Daniel. "Payroll comes due Thursday and we need to pay a boatload of taxes to every agency every government has ever imagined. We're fucked!"

"Listen, drop the drama queen action, Carlito. Human brains, they piss me off. Always a work in progress. Kill me now. How many road cases do you need?"

"Twelve."

"You get eight. Get out of my bar."

I feigned disgust and anger as I left my own fucking bar consoled only with the knowledge Daniel would be sending us $400 million. We didn't need any money. But it's always nice to have a rainy day fund.

The next morning Daniel Tiger showed up in my office and said, "I have terrible news, Patrick. Terrible news."

"No! God no! Please! Don't tell me!"

"Chris is dead."

"Oh. That's too bad, but it's not terrible news," I said as I thought out loud. "I was planning to kill that guy, anyway."

"He killed himself. You're in his will."

"Okay…"

"The good news is, you own half of Idaho," Daniel said.

"Cool! Snake River here I come!"

"The bad news is, Chris never paid any taxes. You might end up with a rowboat, if that."

THE LAST RESORT'S HASTY and unnecessarily lengthy soft opening gave us all a chance to work out the kinks and wrinkles in our operation. Main Street was 100% operational save for artwork inventory in the gallery. I decided we would only sell fine art by living artists to create even more of a cemetery dichotomy. For the cognoscenti. Martin shook his head.

Nik, Royce, and I invited random people we met in the neighborhood (strippers, mostly) to test drive the resort's rooms, restaurants, and rooftop pool. For some reason, they kept coming back. As our guests arrived for the upcoming grand opening celebrations, scheduled to last a month, our crew functioned flawlessly in all areas of the operation. One day, Rainbow Bar & Grill bartender Chauncey told The Last Resort's Operations Manager, Martin, "A man named Gerald wants to speak with you,"

Martin invited Gerald into his office and the two exchanged pleasantries. Martin learned Gerald was the nation's preeminent prognosticator of trends. Gerald smiled and told Martin, "I like what I see here. The whole concept. You're on to something."

"Thanks, Gerald," Martin said. "I hope we make it. We bet our whole business on the Chinese and those customers have disappeared."

Gerald's smile turned to an angry scowl as he scanned the room looking for clues. "Is that the *Wall Shit Journal*? Five dollars a day for bullshit?"

I walked into the resort's lobby and heard a familiar voice in Martin's office screaming about the world's worst newspaper. There's no way it could be—"Motherfucker, you made it!" I exclaimed.

"You must be Black Fucking Patrick," *Trends Journal* guru Gerald Celente said. "Your resort here is incredible, awe-inspiring. I want to live here."

"No, you don't. You'll be dead in a month," I said. "Why don't we host you for a week or three four or five times a year? We'll build you a studio overlooking the resort and make sure you have everything you need to produce your videos and publish *Trends Journal* from here."

"Done."

"You're staying in the Cazadores Suite and we're building a glass cube on top of the amphitheater crypt for your studio. Tell us what you need."

"Wonderful! That's more than I need."

"We need 48 subscriptions to *Trends Journal*. We'll deliver one to every suite every week."

"Done. We appreciate your support."

"Tell us what you want us to stock in your personal wine cellar."

"Wow!"

I took Gerald for a walk up to the roof of the Amphitheater Crypts and showed him the location I had in mind for his studio. "This is amazing," Gerald said. "I'm recording the next episode from my suite tomorrow."

"How?"

"I'll use the webcam thing on my laptop."

"No, you won't."

"Listen you little—"

"Gerald, see all those gigantic buildings down there?" I asked as I pointed down the hill at the huge buildings near the freeway. "Those are all studio rental companies, soundstage facilities, prop houses, everything video production. Dying to get in here, pun intended." I texted the people at the production complex in those big buildings as I told Gerald, "We need a drink."

Amid our second round of martinis, a foursome of film and television experts arrived ready to do business. I suggested Gerald grab a couple of golf carts and tour the facility discussing ideas with the crew, which he did. For some reason, I called Ava.

"Hello Patrick, I miss you," Ava said.

"I know, that's why I'm calling. Where are you?"

"I'm on the Goodyear blimp with Ritchie."

I ended the call and turned my phone off. Blackmore was already in town and conspiring to steal my woman. How does one compete with a man who has the Goodyear blimp on standby at all times? Fuck.

I retreated to the secret bunker behind the secret speakeasy in the semi-secret wine cellar and began various methods of self-pity-aided self-reflection. The overdoses of ketamine and MDMA were just kicking in when the door opened and a blurry Gerald Celente entered. I didn't even ask how he figured out how to bypass the retina scanner.

"Those film people are incredible! They'll be here tomorrow at 6 a.m. to build the Celente Cube!"

"Awesome."

"What's wrong? Patrick? This is the greatest day of your life."

"You wouldn't understand…"

"Fuck you! Have you read the latest *Trends Journal*?"

"Fuck no. Nobody reads anymore. Ritchie Blackmore is stealing my girlfriend, Ava, as we speak."

"Ritchie Blackmore? Fuck that guy. It's Bitchy little Smackwhore. I know Ritchie. Ritchie Blackmore's a bitch. He's the backup bitch Joe Meek called because Jimmy Page was too busy making real records. Fuck that guy."

"Ritchie and Ava are on the Goodyear blimp watching the sunset together right now."

"Oh, shit. I'm so sorry for your loss, Patrick. She's gone."

The power of the Goodyear blimp.

"GERALD, I NEED YOUR HELP. May I show you something only four others on the planet have ever seen?"

"Go ahead, show me your dick. You fucking Californians—"

I told bastard Gerald Celente, "Fuck you. I have an even bigger tool to fuck shit up with," as I led the way into the ultra-secret wine cellar behind the secret wine cellar under the basement of the secret speakeasy.

"You need more storage, there's not even enough room to walk down here."

"No shit. You're looking at almost 200 cubic feet of shit like this," I told Gerald as I lifted the lid on a road case.

For once in his fucking life Gerald was speechless. He looked like he was having a stroke.

"I have fuck you money, Gerald. Serious piles of fuck you cash. I need your help making the most of it."

"200 cubic feet of $100 bills? What the fuck is going on around here?"

"Exactly, Gerald. What the fuck *is* going on around here? What the fuck is going on around here is whatever the fuck we want going on around here. For a long fucking time."

All the money in the whole, wide, wine cellar couldn't make up for the grief I was feeling over the loss of Ava to that pilgrim hat-wearing cunt, Ritchie Blackmore. However, the San Fernando Valley's finest barely-legal pornstars, strippers, and prostitutes helped ease the pain a little. There's a reason we didn't build our cemetery resort in Boise.

"Nik, I've been around the world, tried a million birds. How the hell do you make such amazing fried chicken?"

"My father knew Colonel Sanders. After the Colonel got fucked by corporate America he gave my father the secret recipe."

"No way."

"Then my father got a job at KFC so he could attend their bootleg fast food university, KFCU."

"KFCU?"

"KFCU."

"Fuck."

Armed with the Colonel's secret recipe, documents and anecdotes from KFCU's disgruntled graduates, and historical archives, The Last Resort's scientists developed an aerobic delivery system to spread the smell of Kentucky Fried Chicken, the second greatest scent known to humans, far and wide throughout the San Fernando Valley via its storm drain system. All we did was send more business to KFC. You're welcome, Taco Bell.

Despite all our rage, we couldn't figure out a unique scent to drive business to The Last Resort. Rainbow Bar & Grill pizza didn't work, burgers failed, and anything nautical filled the valley with an even worse valley smell. One day, while we were debating new scents to attempt, Gerald Celente crashed our board meeting. Gerald listened to our bullshit, then looked around the room and asked, "Where's the toilet paper of record?"

Smart guy Martin responded, "It's right there, next to the *Wall Shit Journal*."

Gerald was angry. He stared at Martin and said, "Listen, you little punk. If you'd been reading *Trends Journal* you'd know Korean fucking barbecue is the shit right now. The shit!"

I just looked at Gerald, nodded my approval, and said, "Pho me."

Driving through The Last Resort's rainforest, I confided in Beth, "I have a problem."

"Do you need some dick pills?"

"What? No! But thanks for asking."

"It's okay if you do. Carlito Bandita's machete isn't the same after the estrogen therapy to enhance their rack," Beth shared.

"Wait a minute. You can't just bolt 'em on and it's a done deal? You have to add fertilizer or some shit after the surgery?"

Beth looked at me, shook her head, and said, "Black Patrick, nothing is not easy."

BOOK THREE
SHOWTIME

11
OPEN

ON THE MORNING OF THE LAST RESORT'S Grand Opening Fiesta kickoff, I grabbed Tiko and we went looking for Martin. We found a very pensive, very reflective, very quiet man in the meditation garden. We spent a fortune on that Buddha statue. Martin was elsewhere, living in the past, practicing a useless, outmoded skill on the golf putting green. All of us grieve in different ways.

Time for a pep talk. "You can't have a stool without at least three legs. The three legs of The Last Resort's stool are Tiko, Martin, and me, Black Patrick."

Martin said, "We're adding a drink called the Third Leg to the drink menu in Rainbow Bar & Grill."

Then Tiko asked, "You're not going to go off on some kind of batshit crazy rant today, are you?"

Before the ribbon-cutting, our small group of overachieving gangstas gathered for celebratory drugs and alcohol in the nightclub/event space now known as Three Legs. I felt it was my sacred duty to remind everyone why we were even opening a cemetery resort in Sylmar.

"Motherfuckers! Get mad. Right fucking now! We live in resistance. The ONLY reason we are here is to fuck shit up. Everything we do is designed to subvert societal norms. Not because we're angry—we are. Not because we're victims—we are.

"BECAUSE WE HAVE BEEN *LIED TO! THREATENED! CHEATED! DECEIVED!* Every fucking day of our lives. Our futures were stolen from us by assholes. Fucking assholes! Assholes who broke the social contract. A failed generation who failed to fund education, medication, transportation, recreation. Unlike the many generations that came before them who invested in a fucking future. *WE HAVE BEEN FUCKED!* We owe these old fucks we're burying not one ounce of sympathy. Not one ounce! The old fucks stopped paying taxes in the '70s! Condemning us to a lifetime of shitty schools, traffic nightmares, garbage health care, and no fun. And the cunts tell us we should be grateful for the scraps they've left for us? Shitty schools. No transportation. Poison for breakfast, lunch, and dinner.

"Thank God the evil old fucks continued to fund the incarceration industrial complex, however. The scaredy-cat fucks never blinked a fucking eye when cops asked for more money. For good reason. Where would we be without those brave heroes in the cute little outfits festooned with shiny things and patches designed to delight little boys? Where would we be without those 377 brave motherfuckers we watched watch a classroom or two full of nine and ten-year-olds morph from cute little kids into Swiss cheese and broken teeth strewn all over a blood-soaked classroom floor that day in Uvalde, Texas? Brave heroes! For 77 fucking minutes! Please do salute our courageous last responders. Cowards in costumes. Fuck.

"It's our fault we didn't destroy all of the social constructs we allowed to fuck us in the ass. We let it fucking happen. We get jack shit while everything is handed to the old cocksuckers. We should have French Revolutioned the fuck out of the assholes who stopped paying taxes in the 1970s. The cunts who had their housing costs frozen for the last fifty fucking years. Housing costs frozen for fifty fucking years! And we should be grateful for the shit we live with today? Grateful for what? Grateful none of my friends will live to be 70? Grateful we are all FUCKED because the fucking cunts sold us out to the corporations who fucked up the planet and fed us poison? So the stock portfolios of octogenarians would continue to grow like Warren Buffett's child molesting friend Bill Gates's creep factor? *FUCK* THOSE PEOPLE!. *FUCK* THOSE PEOPLE! Fuck every single fucking one of those motherfucking assholes.

"NONE OF MY FRIENDS FROM HIGH SCHOOL WILL LIVE TO BE 70! BECAUSE THESE FUCKING CUNTS WE'VE INHERITED THE PLANET FROM, WHOSE ONLY JOB WAS TO MAINTAIN THE FUCKING PLANET FOR THEIR MOTHERFUCKING DESCENDANTS, FELT LIKE THEY WERE SO FUCKING SPECIAL WE DIDN'T DESERVE TO LIVE ON THE FUCKING PLANET THEY DID! WE HAVE

BEEN FUCKED! AND IT'S OUR FUCKING FAULT? IT'S OUR FUCKING FAULT. WE FAILED TO WIPE THOSE MOTHERFUCKERS OFF OF THE FACE OF THE MOTHERFUCKING EARTH!"

I caught my breath, inhaled some tequila, and asked, "Any fucking questions?"

"Patrick, why are you so negative?" the recently-repatriated Xyla asked.

"Read the first chapter of *The Confident Man*. Next question."

Royce earnestly wanted to know, "Can I be depressed and angry at the same time without being naked?"

"Survey says… No. Next question."

Mental midget golf guy Martin had to ask, "What about the children?"

"I don't want to offend any of the breeders here. However, I don't give a fuck about your kids. Maybe we should build one of those splash pad things where water shoots up and replace the water with flaming napalm. Next question."

Beth asked, "Can I have more money to buy a few more trees?"

"Beth, please. Slow down. When was the last time you heard 'no' from a man? Of course, you can have more money for more trees. Next question."

"The neighbors are asking for menudo. What do we do about that?" Nik asked.

"Make menudo. Make sure it sucks so they never ask for it again."

"That's impossible. Menudo is terrible, by design. There's no fucking way to make menudo taste worse than menudo already tastes. I'd have to put parts of rotten human carcasses in the stew to make menudo taste any worse."

We all just looked around the room at each other in silence until we couldn't stand it anymore. There is a God. Goddamn that was funny.

LIQUID DEATH AMPHITHEATER AT THE LAST RESORT. IT LOOKS LIKE A BANDSHELL BUT IT'S ONE GIANT SPEAKER.

Our Grand Opening Fiesta at The Last Resort drew huge crowds throughout its run. Live bands, comedy shows, and other festivities in the Liquid Death Amphitheater, our Three Legs club, The Wine Catacomb, and the unnamed speakeasy every night and all day long on weekends. Topless Tapas on The Last Rooftop exceeded all expectations and, more than likely, dozens of local ordinances.

The Outdoor Market at The Last Resort ran the length of Main Street every day and generated significant revenue from our Last Resort-grown produce, merchandise borrowed from

Vallejo, and, our latest venture, Last Resort Barbecue. Rainbow Bar & Grill was slammed every day, cemetery sales exceeded all expectations, the hotel rooms were sold out every night, and a good time was had by almost all. Even The Last Hole golf operation and our crusty old clubhouse, The 19th Hole, kicked ass financially.

Sad and lonely, I stared emptily at the new girl in the flower shop as I longed for Ava. I remembered back to the time when the only reason I ever wanted to start a cemetery entertainment resort was to meet a woman like her. Or Beth—hot, thin, pale skin, death mask makeup, combat boots, barely-there black clothing under an oversized leather jacket. A choker around her neck. An expression frozen in time to commemorate that time her daddy—

"Patrick!" Beth yelled. "Stop being such a creep!"

What the fuck? I didn't even say a word to the new flower-arranger and I was already the asshole. I knew Ava wasn't doing the cockblocking, she was off in an undisclosed location rehearsing gnome music with Ritchie Blackmore. "Fuck you, Beth! Call me when you want to go back to Burger King!"

Nicole may not have been intelligent, but her learning disabilities didn't get in the way of filthy activities. Enthusiastic doesn't even begin to describe her approach to meeting special sexual needs or crafting beautiful displays with cut flowers. That helmet Nicole wore to avoid further brain damage didn't slow her down one bit.

Needless to say, the flower shop benefitted from the special attention and produced fantastic sales numbers at sensational profit margins. As did the entirety of the resort. When we weren't making lifelong, temporary friends at The Last

Rooftop, Martin and I enjoyed watching real-time sales figures compiled by our point-of-sale system. Ticket sales, hotel bookings, burial plots, crypts, wedding venue rentals, flowers, brunch, the outdoor market, Vallejo, golf, booze—our varied and sundry revenue streams were massive.

12
BLACKMORE

THE WEIRD THING ABOUT BLACKMORE'S NIGHT is people gave a shit about Blackmore's Night. We sold out all 28 shows in 90 minutes. Ritchie asked for $1 million more to play two shows with a bootleg version of Rainbow, we said yes. His team asked to use the nightclub venue for VIP meet and greets and fan club bullshit while they were around, and we said yes. Whatever the Blackmore fans wanted, they got. The hotel rooms all sold out and some fans reserved spots in the afterlife in the amphitheater. Whatever the fuck Ritchie wanted, we said yes. It's just easier that way. We pretended we were running a cruise ship without the boat and listeria. Since the neighborhood was full of film and television cunts, Blackmore recorded a handful of shows for release on DVD or whatever format his creepy fans used in their wood-burning stoves.

We probably lost a lot of money, but we put a new cemetery on the map. Nobody can ever take that away from us. And we made a few new friends we're likely spending eternity with by the time you're reading this. One of the many great ideas we came up with during the Blackmore's Night residency: sell future dead people grave markers and tombstones with impressions of their hands, feet, and other body parts/orifices cast in concrete. Like the Chinese theater.

As soon as I saw Ava hit the stage in her hobbit outfit and play her first note I melted. *It's too much*, I said to myself after the opening number ended. I left the amphitheater and went to The 19th Hole where Martin was at the bar eating nachos.

"Dude, we've never seen a night like this. Sales are crazy. Liquor in the front—"

"I quit," I told Martin. "This whole thing is stupid."

"What? This is the culmination of all your dreams! What the fuck?"

"So what? It's all bullshit. Nothing matters."

I drove home, turned my phone off, and spent the next 72 hours snorting various chemical stimulants and playing guitars through stacks of amplifiers at full volume.

I ONLY HAD THE MISFORTUNE to hang out with Ritchie once during the month or so he was in and out of our little cow town. One day he was in the wine cellar with the other goofballs in his band. Those cunts all wore silly elf outfits 24/7, as far as I could tell. While I was leaving the secret walk-in drug safe hidden behind the wall of Cabernet, Ritchie asked me, "Young man, if you were me, would you ever record another album in Montserrat?"

"Ritchie, fuck. It was Montreux," I responded. "While we were building this place, and every single fucking day of my fucking life, I've asked myself one question in times of uncertainty."

RITCHIE BLACKMORE ON THE PHONE WITH GOODYEAR.

"About Montserrat?"
"No, motherfucker. About everything. WWCD?"

"What the hell does that mean?"

"What would Cozy do? What would Cozy do?"

"Cozy would join Black Sabbath. Or hunt down Michael Schenker in whatever insane asylum he's confined to."

"The last thing Cozy would be doing right now is sitting here with a bunch of cunts dressed like goblins. Get your fucking shit together, dude. Burn all of those corny ukuleles and plug your strat into a wall of Marshalls. Fuck you and your Renaissance fair horseshit. Fire all of these little pussies in your silly pirate band and call Foo Fighters. They'll be here in an hour. They'll remind you why the fuck you ever picked up a guitar in the first place. And then you won't look like such a sad fucking twat anymore."

One of the stupid elf weasels in Ritchie's band asked Blackmore, "What's a Cozy?" As the owner of a fractional interest in a cemetery, I wanted to plant that motherfucker right then and there. What has the world come to? Ritchie Blackmore prancing around dressed like a twat with a band of cunts who've never heard of Cozy Powell?

The next day the stranger known as Ava stormed into the secret sex dungeon under the Rainbow while the ghost of Jimmy Bain was teaching me how to write better songs. "Ritchie wants $3 million to play five shows with his new Dave Grohl band, you asshole."

"Trust me. If I killed that banjo band of Blackmore's, I'm the opposite of an asshole. History will look fondly upon me. Ten shows and we have a deal. And we're filming the whole thing for a documentary."

"No. Dave wants to do five small shows here to warm up for the big show at the Forum. He already has a film crew with him 24/7, anyway."

"Dave who? Lee Roth?"

"That's a great idea."

The new and improved version of CPA Chris, CPA Christine, worked out a deal with Foo Fighters whereby The Last Resort would pay Blackmore's Foo Fighters $3 million for five shows. Christine negotiated a few details including five percent of any profits from the documentary film. "We'll never see any of that money," she said. "Movie business accounting makes record business accounting look honest."

"How do we make money, then?" I asked.

"We start rumors Foo Fighters and Ritchie will be buried at The Last Resort one day."

"Fuck. Every guitar player would kill to be buried next to Blackmore."

"No shit. In a road case."

"Fuck! In a road case!"

The sense of satisfaction I felt by killing Ritchie's klezmer band would not last forever, but I savored the moment. Never again would The Last Resort allow a freakish culty, cunty group of posers to invade and commandeer our sacred ground.

Ava reappeared a few days after Foo Fighters absconded with Ritchie. Probably because I begged her to come back.

"Somebody had to do it," I said.

"Do what," Ava asked.

"Kill that leprechaun Grateful Dead bullshit your boyfriend is embarrassing himself with."

"Please, Ritchie's not my boyfriend. He's a narcissistic psychopath who smells like fish 'n' chips. You're the only one I want, Patrick."

"So, what happens next."

"I need to go find my shawm in the pile of gear Blackmore's Night left backstage."

"They left all of their lutes and pirate costumes here?"

"Yes."

There is a God. The Last Resort's First Bonfire turned Renaissance fair instruments into biochar; the drama department at the community college never knew where their semi-authentic Horatio Alger costumes came from. I hope Ritchie had insurance.

13
THE BELL TOWER

Before our opening, we figured out Golden Richards fucked up and neglected to build us a bell tower. What a dick. We fixed that. Somehow, we were able to convince the authorities to allow us to build the world's tallest bell tower. We planted a 444-foot tall tower smack dab at the end of Main Street. Visible for miles around, our tower's manually operated bells would pound out nothing but killer bell music for the masses. And the masses of dead people.

Without warning and on an electric scooter, Esa-Pekka Salonen showed up one day. I didn't know Ritchie and Esa-Pekka were friends. Before long, Ava, Esa-Pekka, Ritchie, and Ritchie's wife were inseparable, entertaining themselves with more stories about Renaissance fair bullshit than opiates could ever wipe from my memory banks.

I showed Esa-Pekka, Ritchie, and Tiger Tower sponsor Daniel Tiger the architectural drawings and artist renditions of the bell tower.

Esa-Pekka sporting a limited edition Black Patrick T-shirt. Like a champion.

"The tower—Esa-Pekka," Ritchie said.
"What?" Daniel asked.
"Esa-Pekka," Ritchie said.
Esa-Pekka said, "Ritchie's saying, 'It's a pecker.'"

"That joke never gets old," Ritchie said. Without a smile or a laugh.

The foreman from the freeway-building company showed up a day later. I could tell he was impressed with himself.

THE WORLD'S GREATEST PLACE TO
WATCH THE SUNSET WITH AN
INTOLERANT ORCHESTRAL
CONDUCTOR. ON ACID.

"How the hell did you dig a 200-foot-deep hole so fast?" I asked.

"We fired bowling ball-sized projectiles of tungsten into the ground with a rail gun."

"Where the fuck did you find a rail gun?"

"The army surplus store. You'd be amazed at what you can find in those places."

"Whatever it takes, we need this thing done yesterday. The bells arrive on a cargo plane from Austria in five days. The bell installers arrive from Hungary five days after that. You have ten days."

"Patrick, here's the timetable we're looking at."

No wonder the freeway overpasses in Sylmar fall down every time there's a hint of an earthquake. I'm pretty sure all I have to do is drive over one of those deathtraps on stilts and say, "EARTHQUAKE," and the creaky bridge will crack in half. The construction companies who build that shit are the least creative and most incompetent motherfuckers anywhere. The king of freeway construction arrived later that afternoon for a meeting, he requested to discuss logistics.

"Gomer, with all due respect. Fuck you. Pour the fucking caissons and build the tower now, before the city and every engineer who's ever seen your bootleg firm's work on an earthquake documentary sounds the alarm."

"We don't have approval to do that, yet."

"Listen, Gomer, get your fuckers here tomorrow morning. I want to see earth moving and rebar cages rising all over the place. No steel, only basalt and fiberglass rebar. We're not CalTrans, we use the good shit."

"That might not happen this week—"

"Gomer, Gomer, Gomer. You stupid motherfucker. My alarm is set for 5 a.m. If I don't see a fleet of motherfucking

Sikorskis dropping material here by 5:20 you are a dead man. A dead man. We're not one of your government clients on a let's-take-ten-years-to-build-a-mile-of-subway timetable. Fuck you. Get it done, motherfucker. Get it done. Now!"

"I'm not sure I can work with a client with your kind of attitude."

I grabbed Gomer by the throat, pinned him against the wall, pulled the Glock out of my waistband, shoved the barrel of the giant pistol in Gomer's mouth, and asked the terrified hard hat-wearing bitch, "Do you want to be sure, or do you want to be rich?"

Gomer stammered and tried to talk but the cold steel tickling his tonsils obscured whatever words he struggled to speak. "You didn't say no. See you tomorrow."

The little bitch named Gomer failed to appear, so Daniel Tiger murdered his housekeeper, kidnapped his kids, and left a note written in blood on the windshield of Gomer's Porsche SUV. What kind of asshole drives a Porsche with more than two doors? "Sikorskis by 11:00 a.m. or you feed the dogs and your kids feed the fish!"

Esa-Pekka took an outsized interest in the bell tower and proposed we create the Esa-Pekka Salonen Institute of Campanology to teach people how to ring bells. Since we couldn't find anybody else who gave a fuck about bells, we agreed to fund Esa-Pekka's pet project. Amazingly. profit margins from the bell-ringing division of The Last Resort exceeded all other product and service categories aside from those undeclared from illegal activities. For a minute. Esa-Pekka was an even bigger dick than Ritchie Blackmore if you can believe that, but his star power attracted aspiring campanologists from near and far. I'm not a doctor, however, don't be surprised if you see a would-be campanologist or two on an episode of *To Catch a Predator* next season

Esa-Pekka's unlimited budget meant we received at least a truckload of bells every day. We had to build a separate warehouse and expand our loading dock to accommodate the mass quantities of bells and mallets rolling into Sylmar every day. At some point the only way to fix the problem was to fire Esa-Pekka but, just like everyone who ever fires Esa-Pekka, the guy never really goes away. Eventually, we gave him a small bell and a cute little outfit and appointed him Town Crier.

14
GUY FERRARI

SELF-SATISFIED BY MY TREMENDOUS PERFORMANCE with the freeway construction fraud/magnate, I took a few days off and went to visit my herd of fighting donkeys in Baja California. On the way to Guy Ferrari's new resort in Cabo San Lucas.

"Guy, what happened with you and Sammy? You guys were perfect for each other."

"Dude, Sammy is a fucking asshole. He only has one friend on the entire planet."

"His bass player?"

"Bingo. Sammy is the typical song-and-dance man. A con artist without the art part."

"What are you?"

"I'm the guy who's made a billion dollars because I have highlights in my hair and wear sunglasses on the wrong side of my head."

FERRARI GUY. AND A MAN WHO CAN'T SWALLOW ENOUGH DONKEY SAUCE.

"Like a more successful version of that Sugar Ray dude?"

"Exactly. Anyway, Sammy tried to fuck me out of my chunk of our tequila company, I told him to eat my ass, lawyers appeared instantly, friendship endship."

"Do you ever think about killing Sammy?"

"Not any more often than anyone else fantasizes about beheading the Red Rocker—maybe three, four times a day."

"Is there anyone you want to kill more than Sammy?"

"I'm not a fan of Taylor Swift."

"Dude! You can't say that! Have you seen those Taylor Swift fan bitches? They are vicious. You can't say that! You're flirtin' with disaster like Molly Hatchet. It's career suicide to talk shit about Taylor Shit."

"Yeah, I know. Her fans are really fucking stupid. And ugly. They need that Taylor Trump cult deal to feel good about themselves."

"I'm not gonna lie, her music is fucking awful."

"You're not gonna lie?"

"I've been waiting a lifetime to start a sentence with that. Pretty cool, huh?"

"Are you on drugs?"

"Does Taylor Swift swallow?"

"Anyway, Sammy says Taylor Swift is worse than Ice Spice."

"Sammy said that? Fuck."

"I have to admit, Patrick, Taylor Swift and her fans do share a certain bond. It's as if there's a special kind of glue that holds them together. I think it's cum. Taylor and her fans are so young, so dumb, and so full of professional athlete cum."

"She should write a song called 'So'"

"Dumb rhymes with cum," Guy noted.

"Call Sammy."

"Michael lives next door."

"Michael can't help us," I told Guy. "Michael has never written a note of music. He didn't even play bass on most of those Van Halen records."

"What did he do?"

"Nobody knows."

15
NDGT

While I was inspecting bell installation at the top of Tiger Tower, a bit of drama unfolded a couple of hundred feet below in Rainbow Bar & Grill. Ritchie and Esa-Pekka were rudely interrupted and immediately displeased by the appearance of a portly fuck who climbed the ladder and sat down uninvited in the Vampire's Lair.

"Get the fuck out of here," Ritchie said.

"Huh, huh, huh, I'm scientist Neil deGrasse Tyson," television personality Neil deGrasse Tyson announced, followed by another round of his moronic, "huh, huh, huh," laughter.

Ritchie wasn't having any of it. "I don't give a fuck if you're astronaut Neil Sedaka, get the fuck out of here before I throw you over the rail, you fucking twat."

Esa-Pekka assured Ritchie he would handle the unwelcome intruder and led Neil out of Rainbow Bar & Grill toward the almost-complete Tiger Tower. "You're a scientist, you say?" Esa-Pekka asked Neil.

Haughty cunt Neil answered, "Of course, I am America's most beloved scientist. You have seen me in—"

"Great, we need help with our bells," Esa-Pekka told the fake scientist.

A MAN STUPID ENOUGH TO BELIEVE WE DON'T NEED TO WORRY ABOUT CLIMATE CHANGE BECAUSE ARTIFICIAL INTELLIGENCE WILL SOLVE IT.

Esa-Pekka knew Neil was a big, fat, out-of-shape, dummy, so he insisted they take the stairs quickly 25 levels up to the belfry. Near-death Neil was a little slow putting on his ear protection as the first note of the 6 p.m. song began at an ear-splitting level of 130 decibels. I observed as the stunned and stupid pseudo-scientist Neil stumbled under the thunder of the first peal. Esa-Pekka helped Neil stabilize himself until he became an angry Esa-Pekka and shoved Neil deGrasse Tyson's head into the larger of the two F# bells as the traditional Sunday performance of Black Sabbath's *Hole in the Sky* commenced. The Last Resort's talented campanologists didn't miss a beat and continued to rock on and ring bells as their ropes were coated by the blood, skull contents, and stench of a dying dumbass. At that moment I knew. I knew Esa-Pekka was the new Johnny Cash—he was killing a man just to watch him die.

As the larger-than-a-football-helmeted head of Neil deGrasse Tyson disappeared in plops and rivers of chunky blood onto and through the floor of Tiger Tower's belfry, I pronounced Neil deGrasse Tyson dead. Neil was an ignorant, stupid, dangerous loser because, for example, he told people artificial intelligence would fix climate change. Really? Fuck you, Neil deGrasse Tyson. Fuck you.

The luckiest of the lucky heard the slightly-deadened sounds the Death Knell of Neil deGrasse Tyson's skull and bones created as the clapper hit the interior and exterior and interior and exterior of his skull before slamming into the 5,000-pound mass of bronze now known as the "The Bell That Sent Neil deGrasse Tyson to Hell." Esa-Pekka commanded the campanologists to play on and on as he fed Neil's torso into the bell. By the time the intrepid bell-ringers were exhausted and ended their rendition of the greatest Black Sabbath song, Esa-Pekka was left holding an ankle sock with a shoe on the end of it and, presumably, a blood-soaked, still quivering, foot inside the ill-advised fashion choice of a loafer NDGT sported as he was executed for crimes against humanity.

We are lucky Neil deGrasse Tyson is dead, cremated, and his ashes buried somewhere he will never be found in the foothills of Sylmar, California. Low IQ Fucktard Neil (LIQFN) needed to eat shit and die long before he met Saint Esa-Pekka. Whenever you see a picture or video containing the painful image of Neil deGrasse Tyson's ugly fucking face, realize you are looking at the face of a stupid fucking cunt. And a sexual predator. I pray you never allowed Neil to give you his signature Native American handshake or let Neil deGrasse Tyson follow your grandma into the ladies' room at a Wendy's.

AVA AND I WORKED AND LIVED next door to each other, but we never saw each other. I didn't want anyone else, Ava was the only one. But a man has needs. She wasn't entirely oblivious to the hookers and strippers Daniel hosted on the hourly. She knew some never made it to the Presidential Suite.

One day I knocked on Ava's door, armed with distractionary conversation pieces harvested from the garden and the not-so-secret wine cellar.

"What's your favorite Ritchie Blackmore song?"

"I can't pick just one," Ava said. "I love the records Ritchie made with Joe Meek."

"Damn…"

Ava saw the shock on my face. "Relax, Patrick. Take it easy."

"Ava, is this real, or isn't it real?"

"It's real. It's real fuckin' real."

"So, we can stop worrying and listen to Zappa?"

"Yes, Patrick. Yes."

"Cool. I'm ordering onion rings."

A MAN NAMED RITCHIE BLACKMORE reappeared in town. Ostensibly to visit Esa-Pekka; probably hoping to steal my girlfriend again. So I took him on the Neil deGrasse Tyson tour. "We have 100 tons of bronze here. And 1,000 smiling knuckles," I told the regal man in the pilgrim hat.

"That's Skin Yard," Ritchie said.

"You are correct, sir. This is a skin yard."

As much as I wanted to hate Ritchie Blackmore, the 50th-anniversary edition of *Machine Head* renewed my faith in the human race. Somehow, some way, thanks to Deep Purple, we would make it out of this deep, dark hole and miserable death spiral people like weak bitch shitty scientist Neil deGrasse Tyson relegated us to. Sorry, ghost of Neil deGrasse Tyson, we're not going down like that. As long as Funky Claude is running in and out, there is hope for us all. Ghost of Neil, shut the fuck up, go back to molesting production assistants. You're embarrassing yourself.

One day, on a stroll through the Long Live Rock 'n' Roll section of the cemetery, as we walked past the wreckage of the Saab 9000 Colin Trevor Flooks crashed at 104 miles per hour in bad weather on the M4, I asked my frenemy, "Ritchie, what's your favorite song?"

Ritchie Blackmore stared me directly in the eye and said, "*I Write the Songs* is the best song ever written."

"The songs of love and special things?"

"I've spent hundreds of hours studying that song. It is perfect, in every way. Absolutely brilliant. The modulations. The modulations!"

"I know it's—"

"The motherfucking modulations!"

100 tons is the weight of your average blue whale. Here's the kicker—nobody's ever seen a blue whale. So, when people tell you something is as big or as heavy as a blue whale, it's a ball of confusion. Don't use that analogy for comparison. Try this: 100 tons is more than 300 pickup trucks. Okay? Fuck you.

A few days later, Esa-Pekka emerged from his bloodthirsty execution situation inspired and on fire. "Esa-Pekka, I pity the fool who challenges your musical authority."

"I hear you, Patrick. I am blessed and grateful to be here with Ritchie and Ava."

"Ava? Ava thinks you're a hack. She's hanging out with Gustavo in Venezuela this weekend."

That comment seemed to incense Esa-Pekka, and I knew he wanted to kill me. Thankfully, Ritchie was lurking in the shadows and broke the tension with his goofy, elfin laughter. Saved my life. Saved my life.

"Fuck you!" Esa-Pekka screamed in my face. "If any of these so-called campologists—"

"Campanologists, Esa-Pekka. Campanologists."

"Whatever. The first fucking time one of these bell-ringing fucks fucks up it's straight into the meat-grinding F# bell."

"Have you thought about trying G? The G bell has some incredible harmonic overtones going for it."

"Stupid. Yes, I have thought about it. I don't want to alter the tone of the G. The F# is about to crack at any time."

"Fuck! Not the F#! That thing's enormous. We had to build the tower around that behemoth. I'm about to be sick."

"Turns out Neil deGrasse Tyson had a bizarrely thick skull. Some say his oyster-rich diet added so much calcium to his bloodstream the circumference of his big, fat skull grew an inch every year. The combination of that and his wig adhesive and leathery skin made his head virtually indestructible."

"Thank God for Black Sabbath."

"Exactly, Patrick. Thank God for Black Sabbath," Esa-Pekka said. A deeply offended Ritchie Blackmore stormed off in anger and was never seen at The Last Resort again. It's not our fault Tony Iommi is a better guitar player.

ESA-PEKKA DEMANDED WE LEAVE the safety of The Last Resort to visit his favorite restaurant in Los Angeles: Barney's Beanery. Since I was high on all the drugs and drunk, Esa-Pekka drove. The hearse. The video I made of Esa-Pekka road-raging at 100 miles per hour in a hearse as he barreled down the 101 freeway headbanging to *Hole in the Sky* remains the TikTok era's greatest accomplishment.

As we scanned the newspaper print menu larger than any newspaper in print, Esa-Pekka confessed, "Patrick, I can't go back to the classical music business. They're all lizard people."

"You're kidding, right? That's a conspiracy theory, isn't it?"

"For once, I wish you were right," Esa-Pekka said, in the most disgusted, insulting way possible.

I tried to change the subject. "It's karaoke night here tonight. You won't believe how many super hot supermodels show up here for karaoke night."

An even more disgusted Esa-Pekka looked up from the extensive chili section of the Barney's menu and disdainfully groaned, "Anybody who excels at karaoke is a lizard person. Why sing other peoples' songs? I find those people lazy and lacking in creativity."

"Haven't you made a career out of performing other peoples' songs?"

Well, apparently, Esa-Pekka took great offense to my equating classical musicians with Shania Twain song-singing karaoke people and roared out of the parking lot of Barney's Beanery in the hearse before our cocaine delivery arrived. Sucks to be him. I ordered a lot.

The glue. The motherfucking glue. My fingers were coated in glue.

"Where the fuck have you been?" the nosy woman at The Last Resort asked.

"I was building a model airplane."

"For three days?"

"Have you ever built a model airplane?"

"No."

"Then shut the fuck up. And you're fired. I don't trust anyone who's never built a model airplane."

Martin emerged from his office and said, "Dammit, Patrick. Quit firing the front desk concierges. As soon as we finish training one and educating her on The Last Resort's amenities you fire her. For no reason."

"Doesn't the community college have a Black Patrick Hospitality scholarship?"

"Yes."

"That means we have an endless supply of talent."

"You're getting a bad reputation over there," Martin reported.

"Because of my huge cock?"

I may have appeared hammered when I re-appeared at work that day. The transcriptions of conversations my clandestine listening devices captured told me words such as intervention, maniac, junkie, drunk, asshole, sex machine, and stroke victim were trending throughout the resort. I found Martin in the meditation garden.

"Martin, I obviously need a vacation. I'm outta here."

"Esa-Pekka's dead."

"Who cares? How's the hearse?" I asked.

"The hearse is fine. That thing's indestructible."

"Good. I'll call you in a week."

It's not my fault Esa-Pekka was a lightweight who couldn't do shots like a champion. And it's not my fault he left before the cocaine arrived, which would have improved his performance behind the wheel substantially.

Like a dog, Ava loved to splay herself out on the cold, hard, concrete floor of the Mermaid Suite naked when she feared overheating, which was every time we were together there, with the HVAC set to 85 degrees Fahrenheit.

"Ava, I'm going to São Paulo for a few days. Did you know, in Brazil, Flor is a popular name for women?"

"Really, Patrick. Tell me more."

"Flor means flower. You are a beautiful flower on the floor not named Flor."

"Fascinating. The end, what a great story."

I didn't need to tell her, but I did. "It's that time of the season to eradicate all foliage. Burn the Amazon down."

"I'm going to kill you."

"Shall I call a Brazilian or a Brazilian to handle the Brazilian?"

The strict no-carpet rule applied to all things The Last Resort touched. The first time anybody said, "Carpet is coming back," resulted in a trip to F# followed by a seat at Royce's chef table in our secret pizza place.

Here he comes again. Daniel Tiger interrupted my breakfast of champions in the secret underground feedback meditation room with, "We need an entrance to the Presidential Suite on the fifth floor."

"Yes, we absolutely do. Tell me more."

"We need a room numbered 526."

"For Lumpyjack?"

"And Wilf."

"And Wilf. Okay. We'll need $50 million for that."

According to CPA Christine, Daniel could never run out of money. If Daniel wanted us to add an entire floor to the hotel because GBH recorded their greatest song about a party in 526 we would make that happen. Christine said Daniel had diplomatic immunity, so anything was possible. Life is easier when you say yes to Daniel Tiger.

"Martin, you need to grab Golden Richards and go see our friends in the planning department."

"You can't be serious."

"You're right about that. However, Daniel wants to add a fifth-floor entrance to his suite."

"Fuck! That will cost us $25 million. It means everything needs to move up. And we'll need to add a sixth floor to the whole resort. And move the roof decks to the seventh floor. The pool, the—"

"Daniel sent me $50 million."

"Fuck yeah! Now it's seven floors of whores!"

16
AVA ACADEMY

STUDENT APPLICATIONS TO THE ESA-PEKKA Salonen Institute of Campanology continued to pour in. Every musician on the planet wanted to study under Esa-Pekka. I guess we forgot to tell people he was dead. You can do that when you own a cemetery. That's a pro tip. The first one's free.

Ava agreed to handle the campanology classes and the community college agreed to lease her the underutilized athletic facility off campus for $1 per year to house the Esa-Pekka Salonen Institute of Campanology. Daniel Tiger suggested we buy the facility, instead, so we used his generous donation to buy the buildings and retool them to house activities more befitting human civilization than team sports. Team sports are for stupid people.

Ava turned the entire complex into a badass music school—Ava Avalon Academy of Music at The Last Resort. The first thing Ava did was launch a courageous initiative to create the best music library in California. Library meaning 100,000 LPs and CDs, 1,000 guitars, 500 amplifiers, 300 keyboards, 300 brass instruments, 100 woodwinds, 200 stringed instruments, drums sets, a dozen grand pianos, P.A. systems. sheet music, books—everything. 5,000 foot pedals! Drum risers, roadies, groupies, managers, agents, engineers, producers, cheerleaders, lighting, mixing desks, tape machines. Luthiers. Microphones, turntables, accordions, upright pianos, electric pianos. Smoke machines. Confetti cannons. Picks, strings, straps, bows, wax, tuners, cables, samplers, video screens, stage props, t-shirt silkscreening equipment and supplies, first aid kits, tour buses. Every DAW and every plugin. Slide whistles. Kazoos. Didgeridoos. Bagpipes. Washboards. Banjos. Slide whistles.

And bells. A shitload of bells. Thousands and thousands of bells of every shape and size imaginable.

A company in decline with a miserable reputation called Amazon approached us and asked how they could help us. We looked at their little website and selected a few thousand items from their extensive catalog, trucks arrived with everything from toilet paper to flamethrowers. Thank you, Amazon.

I dropped into one of Ava's campanology classes one evening. The students in the packed lecture hall were riveted, mesmerized, in fact, by the knowledge Professor Avalon was throwing down.

"Bells hold special powers. Bells offer blessings and promote healing. In times of distress, bells can banish storms and terrify demons. A bell, in the right hands, produces resonant waves with capabilities far beyond our limited comprehension. Bells are magic."

Whoa, that was intense. Every time I saw Ava I wanted her more and more. More than likely, despite all of the Topless Tapas pussy going around, I appeared desperate.

"Patrick," Ava said, "hold the line. Love isn't always on time."

"Toto?"

17
CLOWN TOWN

DANIEL TIGER'S SHENANIGANS AT THE RESORT were attracting complaints from other guests, so I was tasked to convey that message. The prostitute who answered the door of the Presidential Suite 304 announced, "There's something at the door who wants to see you, Daniel." Something? I'm the freak here?

"I don't remember ordering room service. How's the leprechauns-playing-ukuleles for people dressed like pilgrims going?" Daniel Tiger sneered.

"They're gone, but it couldn't have been better. Hey, we're getting complaints about the constant stream of 304s in and out of 304. Can you hire smarter hookers who don't knock on the wrong door every time?"

"Sure," Daniel answered. "When I want ugly ones. Fuck you, Black Patrick." And, with that, Daniel slammed the door. It must be good to be a king.

Later in the day, Daniel Tiger found me in the meditation garden looking for the eight ball I stashed there when I thought we were being raided by the cops.

"Black Patrick," Daniel said with authority, "I'm not prone to apologies."

"Are all of those women hookers?" I asked. "We can get in trouble for that."

"Listen, dummy. You'd be amazed what a woman will do for a $400 bottle of deep conditioner."

"Holy shit! $400 for a bottle of conditioner? How many ounces"

"That's the wholesale price. Listen. My friends want to remove the curse the elf people placed on your little resort here. We're doing a residency here before their big festival in August. Block out the end of July, we start on the 21st."

"What band are we talking about?"

"You'll find out."

Well, so much for quirky classical music, leprechaun banjo bands, and jazz festivals for the first year. Daniel Tiger didn't tell me which band he was talking about—he didn't have to. His Violent J warpaint clearly presaged our upcoming and decidedly legendary week with Insane Clown Posse.

Daniel came back. "By the way, Shaggy 2 Dope called."

"What's a Shaggy 2 Dope?"

"We're hosting the CarJitsu world championship while ICP is here."

"Okay, whatever that is."

INSANE CLOWN POSSE. ALWAYS AND FOREVER MEMBERS
OF THE LAST RESORT POSSE.

"Make sure you have truckloads of Faygo. Faygo. If you run out of Faygo, the Juggalos will burn this whole place down. You need Root Beer, Redpop, Moon Mist, Grape, Faygo in every flavor. Mass quantities."

18
CHINA WALL

The well-behaved and respectful Juggalo crowd's physical appearance and fashion choices scared the shit out of the Chinese Benevolent Association's clients, and everybody else in the neighborhood. To placate some of those traumatized, we agreed to build a separate off-site facility for the Chinese clientele, so we bought a strip mall/shopping center and a couple of its surrounding residential properties two minutes away from The Last Resort.

In no time at all, the strip mall and the houses disappeared and we were left with a 50-foot deep hole in the ground. Golden Richards and the freeway construction company flew in concrete forms, rebar cages, and giant steel beams. Shortly thereafter, a convoy of concrete trucks and pumps roared into Sylmar. Within 72 hours the bones of our two-story temple and banquet facility with a rooftop meditation garden, subterranean parking garage, and underground speakeasy/massage parlor/gambling den took shape.

We hired Nik's recommendation, accomplished financial wizard and seasoned restaurant General Manager, E.D. Park, and his crew from the nearby P.F. Chang they had all worked so hard to put out of business, to handle the off-site China Wall facility. That should have been enough to keep E.D. busy. One day, E.D. showed up and said, "I think we should sell timeshares."

"E.D., fuck you," I replied. "Anytime you meet anyone who says they own a timeshare you run. You're dealing with a stupid person."

E.D. nodded in agreement and said, "Chinese people will pay $500,000 to visit their dead relatives for two weeks every year for 20 years."

"Wait a minute," I told E.D., "you're telling me we can bank $13 million right now and all we need to do is take one hotel room out of circulation?"

"No," E.D. replied, "that's crazy talk. You're not good at math. It's $26 million."

"How many of your Chinese posse want to buy timeshares?" I asked E.D. Park.

"More than a hundred."

"That's at least $100 million! When were you planning to tell me this?"

It was at this point E.D. Park's salary was quadrupled and he received his first six-figure bonus from The Last Resort,

LLC family of companies. And I was won over to the crazy

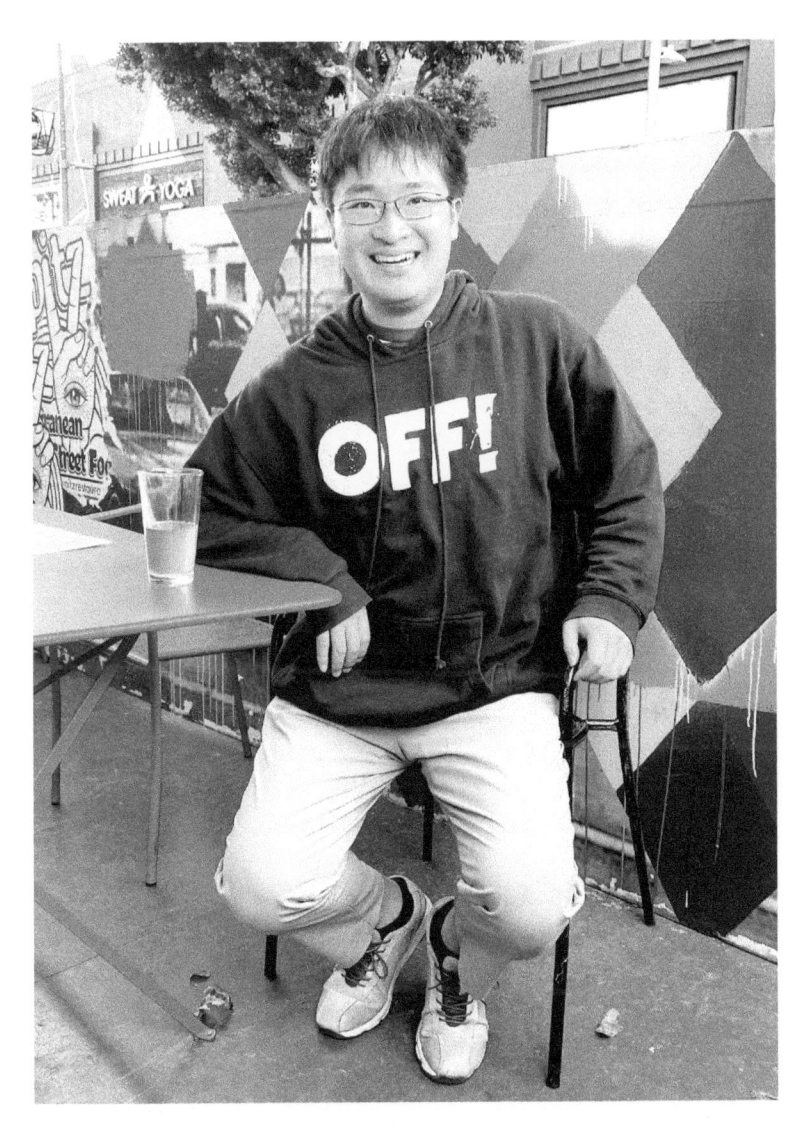

E.D. Park in Little Tokyo. After the jersey swap and right before we were banned from the bootleg kabob place on 2nd Street.

idea to buy some more baseball diamonds and build Chinatown Sylmar. Remember, kids, the ability to admit you're wrong, that your long-held beliefs are bullshit, is a sign of emotional intelligence.

19
I LEFT MY HEART IN....

The Last Resort posse never missed an opportunity to host a raging party for the coeds at the community college. China Wall's grand opening celebration raised the bar. Debauchery off the charts. More than a few of our guests found the secret hiding places hidden amongst the foliage and lion statues in the meditation garden.

Daniel Tiger grabbed an entire platter of fried wontons out of a server's hands and sat down next to me at the bar. "Patrick, this is the best Chinese restaurant I've ever been to. E.D. Park is a fucking genius. Did I pay for this?"

"Not yet, I sent you an invoice…"

"I'll send you the money but you need to change the name."

"Tiger's?"

"Fire Tiger."

"Done."

Fire Tiger was a far better name than China Wall. P.F. Chang veteran E.D. Park agreed, Golden Richards got to work designing a new logo, full speed ahead.

My neglected trophy date poked me in the forehead. She didn't use her finger. "Ava, Happy Birthday, you are the love of my life. You make every day like Christmas."

"I won $2,000 playing sic bo in the casino."

"What the hell is sic bo?"

"I have no idea," Ava answered. "I rolled dice, people cheered, and then they gave me cash."

"Congratulations, beautiful. We're flying to the wine country tomorrow morning."

"Yes, we are."

Ava and I landed in Santa Rosa and went straight from Charles M. Schulz–Sonoma County Airport to the Charles M. Schulz Museum and Research Center—Ava's enthusiasm for cartoon character Snoopy was weird but mostly manageable most of the time. I didn't expect to see Ava cry so much at the sight of Snoopy images and merchandise, however. Once our trip through the gift shop Ava practically cleaned out was complete, we hit the road for a wine-tasting tour.

At Ava's Snoopy-themed birthday dinner in our Healdsburg-adjacent hotel's restaurant, the birthday girl told me, "Daniel Tiger says there's a portal to the underworld in your cemetery."

"Cool."

"No, it's not cool at all. The way Daniel describes it, the underworld is an underground city with houses, stores, schools, transportation—everything people ordinarily have, except it's underground."

"Daniel eats a lot of mescaline."

"No, that's not it. He showed me pictures and video of tunnels and bizarre things going on down there. I don't want to go back to Sylmar."

"Works for me. Where would you like to go first, Ava?"

"I don't know. There's no safe place anymore. The lizard people—"

"Lizard people?"

"Yeah, sounds crazy, huh?"

"A little."

"Daniel's a lizard person."

"He is?"

"Yeah. How do you think he's so wealthy? It's all the lizard people buying his lizard shampoo on QVC."

"Everybody knows that."

"No, stupid. They've been manipulating us and grooming us for thousands of years. Something major is about to happen, according to Daniel."

"C'est la vie, mi amour. You're even more beautiful in Geyserville than you are in Sylmar." Hot librarian, Ava, stared and stared at me in silence for an uncomfortably long time. "We're staying here as long as you like, beautiful. Unless you want to go to the Tonga Room in San Francisco. It rains indoors and thunder erupts randomly in there, sometimes."

Ava responded with words she would soon come to regret. "We don't get to spend enough time together, Patrick."

After a couple of days, the cocaine paranoia wore off and Ava expressed a desire to return to her eponymous school and library, so we bid a fond farewell to the grape-stomping people, vowing to return again soon. I can't say I was necessarily unhappy to end our brief getaway. If I had to hear one more crazy story about those lizard people...

I CALL HER AVA KNAVEL SOMETIMES.

The plane ride from San Francisco to Burbank was a white-knuckler. A roller coaster with tiny bottles of tequila and screaming flight attendants. Brutal winds—Devil Winds, in the local vernacular—tossed our little Southwest 737 around like a motherfucker for the duration of the flight. I wish I hadn't heard one flight attendant tell another flight attendant, "The captain shit his pants." That's no way to inspire confidence in a pilot.

Ava and I decided to spend the night at The Last Resort. Cute young couple Royce and Xyla joined Ava and me in the V.I.P. Room (Very Insecure People) at Rainbow Bar & Grill for a nightcap. Royce and Xyla now occupied the caretaker's house at The Last Resort.

"Something's going on around here," Royce said. "We're hearing strange noises at random times and the ground shakes."

"Pussy. Does it scare you?" I asked. "We almost died on an airplane today."

Xyla said, "Ava, I feel your pain." Then, "Fuck you, Patrick. We hear fighter jets, loud as fuck, but there are no airplanes in the sky."

"Are you guys on drugs?" I asked.

"Of course, we are," Royce said.

"Birds fly upside down laughing," Xyla said. "It rained this morning then all of the raindrops reversed course and fell back up into the clouds."

Smart ass Ava said, "Video or it didn't happen."

Well, both Royce and Xyla were armed and ready with multiple, astonishing clips of inexplicable upside-down rainfall activity.

"The reverse thunder and lightning is badass," Royce revealed.

"Has anybody else seen this shit?" I asked.

Royce answered, "It's happening all over the world. There are hundreds of videos on YouTube."

"And PornHub," my ex-girlfriend, Xyla, added. She learned so much from me.

Royce bore nothing but bad news, "Business is suddenly terrible. All of our Chinese funerals are canceled. The lunar calendar is blank."

"The lunar calendar? Blank? Fuck! That's not good. That's not good at all."

I didn't even want to know about the Mayan calendar. I took solace in the fact the calendar most people use is a bullshit construct of a child-molesting pope named Gregory, hence the moniker, Gregorian. When Black Patrick gets around to fixing all of the errors in our daylight savings time bullshit, time will be denoted using the Black Patrick calendar. Which will be black as fuck.

It was time for a pep talk. "I need to let you guys know something. When I told people about my idea for a five-star cemetery resort, they all said I was crazy. They were wrong. Really fucking wrong. We will ride this storm out. Like REO Speedwagon."

"What about the $400 million in the not-so-secret wine cellar?" Ava asked. "Why don't we take the money and run if this is a sinking ship?"

What the fuck? Ava doesn't even work here. "Yes. We could do that with the $395 million in the wine cellar, but we don't run, we stand our ground. We fight."

"What happened to the other $5 million?" Royce asked.

"I paid a guy to shoot down a blimp."

Ava's fantasy about geographical relocation failed to end the lizard people conspiracy theory bullshit coming out of that hole in her face. Ava looked at me like I was stupid and said, "Daniel is the king of the lizard people," as she bent over the counter in the bathroom and removed her warpaint. "All of the crazy shit Royce and Xyla are talking about is Daniel and his lizard people."

Confused, as usual, I exclaimed, "What?" as I noted the crazy ones are, indeed, better in bed.

"Beth and Carlito Bandita are high-level lizards."

"No fucking way."

"Way. You've surrounded yourself with lizard people."

"Whoa, so that's why Daniel lives here and not in one of his mansions…"

BOOK FOUR
BOOMING BUSINESS

20
THE EXPLOSION

Ava and I were wiped out from her birthday getaway, so we slept in. At 9:09 a.m. we were thrown out of the bed by a massive jolt and slammed onto the epoxy-coated distressed concrete floor. The room rocked and bounced around for what felt like forever as everything not nailed down hit the floor all around us. I didn't know where the hell we were or what was happening; Ava was screaming in several languages.

Once the shaking lessened to cruise-ship-in-a-hurricane levels, which took a while—The Last Resort was built on rollers, rubber pads, springs, and had massive concrete counter-balancing blocks of concrete suspended on wire cables hanging hundreds of feet underneath it—Ava and I crawled out on the balcony to survey the battered planet outside. To the west, walls of fire and thick, black smoke rose from the ground and moved across the land heading away from us, driven by the hot, dry Santa Ana winds. Fortunately for us, and unfortunately for millions of San Fernando Valley residents, we were upwind of the firestorm poised to kill everything in its path from the East San Fernando Valley to the Pacific Ocean. "Today's going to be wild," I said to Ava.

A groggy and hungover Ava asked, "How do we stop those fucking bells?"

We collected ourselves, ran downstairs to ground level, and found a few dozen people in various states of shock. Ava jumped in a golf cart to go see what her music school looked like, I took a hike around the property to assess the damage. Sprinklers and fountains were active throughout the resort property. Everything we built in the last couple of years looked fine. The relic known as The 19th Hole was totally wrecked, no big deal.

Car alarms wailed. Distant fires and smoke were visible in every direction. Explosions rocked the ground every 20 minutes or so for a couple of hours—thankfully each sounded further and further away. Until one, massive explosion knocked me off my feet as a mushroom cloud of fire rose miles into the sky and the population of Porter Ranch met its demise. What kind of moron lives on top of the world's largest natural gas storage site? None, after that day.

By noon the property was a ghost town. Every guest left in a panic, and all of our staff members ran home to check on their families. Xyla and Royce were around, as were Nik and his wife, Nikki. Dee and D.D. remained on site. Martin was nowhere to be found. Beth and Carlita Bandita were gone. Daniel Tiger's suite was empty and filled with guns and ammunition, for some reason. Ava roared back into the resort on her golf cart with bad news about the music facility.

"The music school is history. Almost everybody's dead around here. The few people still alive are looting everything, they're headed this way."

Well, thanks to our fencing, moat, and Daniel Tiger's leftover stash of machine guns, rocket-propelled grenade launchers, night vision goggles, body armor, and fireworks, we were able to repel the zombie looters all afternoon until packs of newly wild dogs started roaming the streets of Sylmar looking for dinner.

POST-EXPLOSION FIRESTORM. BEFORE IT KILLED ALMOST EVERYONE IN SYLMAR.

Once things seemed to calm down a little bit, Royce and Nik launched drones to survey the local landscape. A huge, blown-out trench separated our little part of Sylmar from the rest of the planet—a trench that followed the exact route of the tunnel being dug at the time of the 1971 Sylmar Tunnel Disaster. The trench line delineated our side of Sylmar from the apocalyptic hellscape downwind where no movement or signs of life were anywhere to be seen. Up the hill in the opposite direction, behind The Last Resort, in Sylmar's most affluent, gated community, a few homes remained intact with people huddled around bonfires.

Nik, Royce, and I hauled guns and ammo to the top of the bell tower and set up an observation post high above the compound. Nik asked, "What's the plan, Black Patrick?"

"We need to work in shifts guarding this fucking place until help arrives. Sooner or later whoever's left around here will get hungry and figure out we're still here. Do all of our cameras still work?"

"Everything works," Royce said. "The motion-detecting lights, the cameras, the walls and fences held up—it's all good."

"What about the food, Nik?" I asked.

"All is well. Tomorrow I'll make sure whatever we can freeze is in a freezer. And we need to dig through the rubble of The 19th Hole and see what's in there."

"What's up with all the dogs?" I asked, above the din of hundreds of dogs barking.

Nik answered, "They're hungry."

"We should feed 'em," Royce said. "They can't get in here, but we can keep 'em close."

"Do we want to give dogs our food?" I asked.

A wise man named Royce said, "No. We don't feed them people food. We feed them people, as food."

And that's how we turned every feral animal in the neighborhood into our loyal, vicious, flesh-eating, perimeter defense force.

21
LIZARD PEOPLE

THANKS TO THE POWER OF ALTERNATIVE pharmaceuticals, Royce, Nik, and I remained awake, alert, and on patrol throughout the night. As the sun rose and our fellow survivors took positions on guard, we took a break to drink breakfast and dig through the wreckage of The 19th Hole. Underneath the flattened building we found little of value save for canned food, beer, some booze, and a lot of destruction. Nik pulled an old-fashioned telephone out of a pile of golf trophies and, as a joke, put the receiver to his ear. "Hey, it has a dial tone!" Royce and I kept digging, assuming Nik was kidding around. "This phone works!"

Our mobile phones didn't work, but we had our contacts stored in them, so we took turns calling the numbers of people we thought might have landlines, which was almost nobody. I remembered an old friend, Melissa, who worked for the USGS in Northern California, so I called her, and she answered.

"Hey, it's Black Patrick. Remember that time we were in that earthquake in San Francisco?"

"Where are you?"

"Sylmar. We run a resort and cemetery here on top of an old golf course. You should come visit sometime. Insane Clown Posse was just here a few weeks ago."

"Oh, no. Have you seen the news?"

"No, we don't have TV stations here anymore."

"It's a global thing."

"What does that mean?"

"What's being reported as an earthquake happened everywhere. At the same time. Worldwide. It wasn't an earthquake."

"What was it? It felt like an earthquake, to me."

"Are you sitting down?"

"You're not going to tell me you're a stripper again—"

"Shut up. The lizard people blew everything up on their way out of town. Everything. Their entire underground civilization, boom!"

"That's not good."

"The Earth is, well, was, hollow. Sylmar was the main headquarters of the lizards—the last stop on their highway from the Denver airport through the four corners and Grand Canyon under the Volcano House to the massive complex under your golf course. From there they went to their underwater Malibu facility, boarded enormous spaceships, and shot out into the middle of the Pacific. Then, onward. First to their transfer station inside the hollow moon, then, to infinity and beyond."

"How do you know all of that shit?"

"My husband works for NASA. That's what he says, at least. I'm pretty sure he's a secret agent of some kind. The fucked up thing is, all of the crop circles people dismissed as hoaxes were messages clearly indicating exactly what was going to happen."

"We'll know better next time. What happens next?"

"Most of your friends are gone forever. You'll be led to believe they died in an earthquake—that's total bullshit. They were lizard people and they're on another lizard planet by now."

"Bummer."

"Every methane deposit sequestered in the earth ignited when Lizard land exploded, sending flames into the air all over the planet at the same time. After that, everybody in California who didn't fry in a fire drowned in a tsunami, as far as we can tell. That's the rest of your friends. The tsunamis are still wiping out beach people."

"Great! Beach people suck."

"Human civilization is toast. In a week everybody left will be cannibals."

"Perfect. We have a freezer full of dead people. What's next? Zombies? Mothra? Godzilla?"

"All of the above. You're going to die. Find a couple of friends and start partying."

"We have a bunker, a restaurant full of food, a wine cellar full of booze, hundreds of millions of dollars in cash, and more drugs than CVS and Pablo Escobar combined."

"I guarantee you, all of your food and booze will be gone as soon as your neighbors run out of corpses to eat. If you have a place to hide, go there now."

As instructed by my geologist, I made a beeline to the secret wine cellar behind the secret wine cellar inside the wine cellar. The secret wine cellar bunker was known to myself, Martin, and Daniel Tiger only, so it came as a surprise to find Ava and Xyla behind the wall of Cabernet. Speechless, for many reasons, I stood in astonishment as the blast door closed behind me.

"Who told you about my secret bunker?" I asked.

"You talk in your sleep," Ava said.

"A lot," added Xyla.

I told Ava and Xyla what Melissa told me. What happened was not an earthquake, it was a global explosion caused by the reptilian humanoids blowing up their entire underground world. Melissa was astounded to hear we were still alive as Sylmar was revealed to be the home of the Lizard People leadership.

"I told you," Ava said.

"The good news is, all the cops were lizard people, so we don't have to deal with those losers, anymore."

"What about the billionaires?"

"All gone."

"So, we have to cancel this year's *Kill a Billionaire Extravaganza*?"

"Over ten million cops, cop supporters, cop family members, security guards—gone."

"Who else?"

"Tow truck drivers, politicians, bankers, CEOs, CFOs, psychopaths, sociopaths, athletes and coaches, stockbrokers, actors, nazis, warlords, religious fanatics, terrorists, murderers, rapists, child molesters, landlords, Bayer/Monsanto employees"

"I get the picture. Thank you, Ava. Melissa told me Antarctica blew up and tsunamis are circling the globe.'

"Duh."

E VERYONE BUT ME SEEMED TO KNOW something about the lizard people. Royce found me in the bar at Rainbow Bar & Grill and told me, "Beth programmed all of the sprinklers to start blasting everything with mass quantities of water starting an hour before the planned detonation of the underworld. That's the main reason most of our vegetation survived."

"Any damage in the crematorium?"

"No, we're good, The 19th Hole is our only casualty, but that's no big loss. Martin won't be back."

"Aww, fuck. He was a lizard?"

"Still is," Royce said as he shifted gears. "We're about to get real busy around here. I flew my drone over the freeway—it collapsed."

"Again?"

"Of course it did, it's in Sylmar. All of the buildings on the other side are flat, charred, and smoldering. Everybody died."

"Vallejo?"

"Toast. There were two million people in the San Fernando Valley before the blowout. At least 50% of those are dead, probably a lot more. We're about to make a fortune."

"Who's going to pay us to bury everyone?"

"The feds. That's all they're good for. We need more excavators. I'll be digging graves 18 hours a day, every day, starting right now."

"We're not wasting our time burying people. Fuck that. All our peeps good?"

"Fire Tiger is still standing but nobody's seen E.D."

22
LAST STAND

I MUST HAVE PASSED OUT in the meditation garden. At precisely 9:09 a.m. Ava shook me awake and said, "Everybody's waiting for you on the rooftop. We need to have a meeting."

"I had a nightmare the world exploded."

Everybody in my world was waiting for me on the rooftop pool deck. That amounted to me and five other people: Ava, Royce, Xyla, Nik, and Nik's wife, Nikki. And maybe Dee and D.D. All any of us had left was each other. And mass quantities of drugs, alcohol, food, and cash.

The first thing we did was talk about how we were going to stay alive. Our little compound was remarkably secure, self-contained, and self-sufficient. However, we determined to work 12-hour shifts patrolling the perimeter of The Last Resort, monitoring the security cameras, and flying drones around the neighborhood to keep an eye out for potential cannibals.

Next, we took an inventory of basic necessities. We determined we had plenty of water in storage tanks, ponds, and our groundwater wells to keep our people, animals, and plants alive.

Rainbow Bar & Grill's massive basement freezers and pantries contained enough food to feed a thousand people for a year. Our food forest, chickens, and fish farm operation would crank out more than we could consume.

Solar power and giant propane tanks would power everything for years and years. Guns, ammo, and guard dogs would keep us safe.

Oh, yeah. I almost forgot. We had thousands of cases of every kind of booze and a shitload of drugs.

We soon came to the realization Martin, Daniel, and Xyla had prepared us to survive the adversities our future had in store.

The greenhouse was full of seedlings and saplings sprouting—fruits and vegetables but very few flowers. Tons, and tons of seeds, compost, and soil.

As we dug into the food storage it was clear Martin had loaded up every freezer, pantry, and storeroom with massive amounts of non-perishables on his way out. And the hotel area of the resort was overloaded with toiletries, cleaning supplies, and everything we might need in bulk.

In addition to the massive cash stash and the arsenal in the Presidential Suite, Daniel left behind enough guns, ammunition, and combat gear to fight a small civil war—machine guns, hand grenades, flame throwers, night-vision goggles, drones, you name it—in his private club underneath the caretaker's house.

A couple of dozen people we could trust survived in the immediate area around The Last Resort. Some would bring food, ammunition, drugs, propane, booze, livestock, and other items they had scavenged or looted. We bought everything and paid our trusted suppliers very handsomely with our unlimited cash on hand. Especially the guy who looted the pharmacy at the hospital.

When the morgue's freezer ran out of human thigh bones, Royce started digging up dog food from our human garden. For months we guarded the property in 12-hour shifts and kept a low profile so as not to attract the cannibals we could hear howling in the night. We were so bored we started paying the local scavengers thousands of dollars each for puzzles and board games. Our twice-daily 9:09 meetings at shift change were inevitably downers with at least one of us threatening to kill ourselves every week.

At our collective low point, when the future looked hopeless for all six of us, a dramatic event shocked us out of our depression. The brown tint in the skies above Sylmar turned from brown back to the blue we once knew, and a gold 1970s Chevy Impala with white interior crashed into the fence surrounding The Last Resort. Three human figures silhouetted in the black smoke of the burning car emerged into view as the car exploded in a mushroom cloud, repairing the hole it made in our fence.

Stationed on the observation deck of Tiger Tower, I was a millisecond away from opening fire with the sniper rifle when I recognized the driver. It was E.D. Park. With Dee and D.D. in tow.

"Dude, you're alive! We thought you were dead. What happened to your face?"

"I was driving down the freeway and my car went flying when the freeway collapsed, again."

"What are the odds? Where have you been?"

"Fire Tiger. Everything was cool there until Dee and D.D. got tired of Chinese food. So we came back."

"Glad you're okay. We thought you were a lizard person."

"I am. I missed my flight to the moon. I was running late…"

And that's how E.D. became the last remaining lizard person on the planet.

WE LEARNED A LOT FROM E.D. PARK during his torture and interrogation. Turns out Daniel Tiger was cloned from the genetic combination of Lizard King/worst vocalist in history, Jim Morrison, Hitler's Pope, and whatever else the mad lizard scientists put in a blender and implanted in one of decapitated actress Jayne Mansfield's leftover eggs.

Illuminati on the moon transmitted a blocking frequency to keep us from seeing what was in front of our faces our entire lives in order to enslave us. Martin led a secret life as a shapeshifting fascist pedophile lizard Satanist.

Good times.

BOOK FIVE
THE SPECIAL GUEST

23
WHO ARE YOU?

AFTER MONTHS OF AIRCRAFT INACTIVITY IN THE SKIES above The Last Resort, we observed silent black helicopters hovering above us. Airplanes appeared in the skies, once again. Drones, too. We knew we were being watched. By whom?

One morning a small, single-seat black helicopter hovered low over the Veterans' cemetery and fired a lawn dart into the ground in front of the chapel. "Read the note," the pilot announced over a speaker, then the helicopter flew away.

We were all afraid it was some kind of trick or a booby trap, so we slammed multiple shots of Jaegermeister, said "Fuck it," and Nik drew the short straw. Nik yanked the dart out of the ground, unscrewed the tail section, and pulled out a rolled-up piece of parchment. The note inside said, "I look forward to seeing you maniacs for lunch tomorrow. What's the soup de jour? All the best, your President."

"What the fuck does that mean?" Royce asked.

"It sounds like our president is expecting soup tomorrow, whoever that is." I conjectured.

"Okay, what do we do?" Nik asked.

"If it's the President of the United States or California, or wherever it is we live now, they won't be traveling alone. So we prepare a state fucking dinner-level banquet for a lot of people."

"How do we know it's the president and not the lizard people?" Royce asked.

"It's not the lizard people," E.D. said, "trust me."

The whole gang retreated to Rainbow Bar & Grill to freak out, plan the menu, and delegate responsibilities. Turns out Nik stashed a boatload of dry-aged ribeye in anticipation of just such a special occasion. The fish in our largest pond were quite delicious, so E.D. went fishing and brought back a couple of hundred pounds of fresh fish for our legendary Rainbow Bar & Grill Grilled Rainbow Trout. Royce slaughtered a dozen of our healthiest chickens. Then there was the pasta with fresh vegetables, garlic, and olive oil. Grilled asparagus. Margaritas. Mashed potatoes. Mixed greens salad. Fresh fruit. Coffee. Tea. Champagne. Beer. Wine. Tequila. The Last Resort's Famous Cheesecake.

As Nik assembled ingredients and cooking utensils, Xyla and Nikki went farming, Ava, Dee, and D.D. gathered all of the necessary service items, cutlery, and glasses, and set up the Presidential Suite as a banquet room. I assembled all of the beverages and set up the bar. Once those tasks were accomplished we all took a break to relax and agreed to reassemble at 5 a.m. to do some gourmet cooking.

Nik was ready to rock when everybody groggily entered Rainbow Bar & Grill before sunrise on D-Day. A small round table sat just outside the kitchen entrance with a pizza platter on top and a dome covering. Nik said, "Good morning everyone! Today will be a blast. Before I start in on the details, let's begin here." With that Nik lifted the dome revealing the large pizza platter overflowing with cocaine. "I recommend the cocaine and coffee combination. And a shot."

We all started the morning's cocaethylene party with gusto, Nik gave us all our marching orders, charcoal aflame, produce chopped, fish filleted, and more. With everybody firing on all cylinders and the sun coming up, we were suddenly surrounded by a dozen men and women in black suits wearing sunglasses. How they appeared out of nowhere without warning remains a mystery. These sneaky people were the President's advance team, some remained in the kitchen to watch every step of the food preparation process and grill (sorry) Nik on the origin of the food. Others surveilled every inch of the property. We learned drugs were now legal. Soldiers with machine guns set up a perimeter around the property. Giant helicopters dropped bulldozers and shipping containers all over the place outside our compound. Drones, fighter jets, the whole nine yards. A helicopter arrived with personnel to finish food preparation and provide service to the luncheon guests. We were left, as a group, with nothing to do for a few hours for the first time in months.

All of us wanted to know what the fuck was happening. A guy who seemed to be in charge of everything and everybody supervised our visitors and told us the President would arrive in two hours, so we should clean up. We retreated to our rooms and made ourselves presentable.

I needed more cocaine so I took a quick shower, put on my best leisure wear, and headed back to the Rainbow. I inhaled some of Nik's stash, offered the assembled executive types some scotch, and sat down for a chat.

"Who's the President," I asked the guy in charge.

He chuckled, and answered, "It's a surprise."

"What's he or she President of?" I asked.

"You'll find out," he said. "Do you guys need anything here?"

"Protection. We're all exhausted from keeping an eye on this place 24/7. I feel like we're about to be invaded here any minute."

"You were. We've been watching this place. The natives are restless. There was a very close call a few days ago. Very close."

"Well, that makes me feel better."

"We don't know where they got the tanks. Anyway, you have more protection than you could ever imagine, now. Relax. The President's 90 minutes out. You're going to shit when you see him."

"I'm sure I will."

"He asks about you guys every day in our morning briefing."

"That makes sense if he's the president of Forest Lawn. You can't give me a hint?"

I walked outside to get some air and there were dozens of new arrivals. Helicopters were in and out disembarking staffers, photographers, and equipment—total insanity. I swear I saw scuba divers in the ponds. I was staring at the sky attempting to understand it all and to keep the cocaine drip from running out of my nose and down my face when I felt a pair of soft, moist lips before sharp teeth bit my earlobe.

"You must be hungry," I told the world's most beautiful and talented woman.

"Starving," Ava said.

"Did you ever have this much fun before you met me?"

"Yes," Ava responded, "but it was a different kind of fun."

"A different kind of fun. I'm writing that one down."

"Five minutes," the guy in charge said as fighter jets roared over The Last Resort at bell tower level disappearing in a scream and cloud of afterburner exhaust.

"Is this fucker coming in on a UFO?" Nik asked. "This is bonkers."

Three massive helicopters approached from the east—the President always travels in one of three identical choppers so nobody knows which one to shoot down. After a couple of slow laps around the resort, all three touched down simultaneously on the landing pads the special forces laid down earlier in the day. A few dozen more people exited the helicopters, Ava and I were wondering which one was the President. We surmised it wasn't the film crew he was traveling with. Or any of the guys with machine guns. The President's entourage walked into the middle of Main Street while the residents of The Last Resort and the guy in charge waited to see if anybody else was joining us. Megan Fox and Machine Gun Kelly walked off a helicopter. "Is Machine Gun Kelly the President?" I asked the guy in charge, who didn't answer. Then, an even hotter woman than Megan Fox, something scientists had previously declared a physical impossibility, stepped off the helicopter followed by an old friend of ours.

This must be some really good acid, I thought to myself as I stood frozen and speechless. The rest of The Last Resort crew were jumping up and down, laughing, screaming, clapping, hugging, high high-fiving. The President greeted everybody, I was last.

I asked the President, "What the fuck is going on around here? How the hell did this happen?"

"It was all in *Trends Journal*," said the ever-ebullient President Gerald Celente. "What's for lunch?"

A group of maybe 30 of us were led to the Presidential Suite while the remainder of the President's massive touring party feasted on pizza and other pre-explosion delicacies in the Rainbow Bar & Grill. With champagne glasses full, President Celente rose to give a speech.

"I'm starving and I know everybody in this room has been working really hard on very little sleep, so I'll make this brief. The last nine months and nine days since The Explosion have been the worst in human history. Thank you all for your hospitality here at one of the very few pockets of civilized survivors left on the planet. I will be here for three or four days and can't wait to catch up. Cheers!"

And, with that, we dove into the most amazing meal any of us had ever enjoyed. Ava was seated next to Megan Fox and I have no idea what they were doing to each other and planning for later. Xyla got totally hammered and started crawling around under the table. E.D. Park finished his meal quickly and excused himself to converse with a member of Gerald's staff. Royce smiled for the first time, I think. Dee and D.D. started a small food fight with themselves. Nik and

THE GREATEST. YOU CAN'T TOUCH THIS. YOUR
PRESIDENT CELENTE

Nikki were in a state of shock and loved every minute of it. Photographers and the President's film crew captured the entire scene. As coffee and dessert were served, the new guy in charge tapped me on the shoulder and said, "Come with me." He led me to the elevator and said, "I'm President Celente's Chief of Staff, Joe Garagiola, thank you for having us."

"Who's paying the bill," I joked as we waited in the elevator whose doors remained open, violating the laws of physics. Gerald joined us, we hit the ground floor and strolled down an empty and silent Main Street.

"Let's hit the bell tower, I need to get my stairs in.," President Celente said. "Megan's cousin is a handful."

Gerald wanted to ring a bell, so we stopped in the bell-ringing chamber. "Which one of these ropes do I grab? I want one, solid ring."

"The red one," I answered. "We haven't rung a bell or made a sound here since The Explosion. We've been lying low."

"I know." Gerald grabbed the rope and gave it a solid yank, a slightly distorted, slightly flat F# rang out loud and clear across the San Fernando Valley.

We stepped out onto the observation deck and surveyed the wreckage of California. Gerald said, "Four billion were lizards. The lizards took a billion humans with them for slaves and meat. Two billion died in the explosions, fires, and floods. The people left here after that started killing each other. We think there are less than 5,000,000 people alive on Earth and most of those are totally fucked-up."

"What are you President of?"

"Everything."

"Everything?"

"Everything that's left. That's not very much. I need a few days to think. None of us have left the capital since we put all this shit together."

"Where's the capital?"

"Omaha. Every city on the coasts, anywhere, was completely wiped out. Along with *all* the people."

"I'll bet…"

"The good news is, a lot of very intelligent and capable people survived. We won't go all the way back to caveman days. Sadly, things won't be pretty for a long time…"

"What are your plans while you're here?"

"We're turning this place into a fortress. You have a permanent military presence here; everything within a one-mile radius is locked down and walled in. My people are going to learn everything about your model here so we can roll it out in other places. Ironically, by wiping out most of human civilization, we've managed to save human civilization. No more cars, airplanes, or bullshit jobs. Nobody's overfishing the oceans, there's no factory farming or massive livestock activity, and nobody's logging on an industrial scale. Sure, there's a lot of damage and the oceans glow at night, but we'll be okay."

"Why's Machine Gun Kelly here?"

"Because Megan Fox comes with. Can we have Machine Gun perform in your amphitheater tomorrow night?"

"Do we have to?"

"You're the President of California, now. You decide if you want to watch his wife on a stripper pole."

UNBEKNOWNST TO ANY OF US, the President's crew organized a poolside after-dinner party then an all-night rager in Three Legs. Before that, Joe Garagiola directed everyone to the amphitheater for a televised Presidential press conference. Photographers, seated reporters eager to ask questions, a lectern, the whole deal. Gerald greeted "the people," said some inspirational words about transcending adversity, plugged the new edition of *Trends Journal*, answered a few questions from reporters, and then said, "It is my great honor to introduce the President of California, President Black Patrick."

What a dick. I didn't know what to say to anybody, let alone the remaining few people on the planet with some type of operating communication device. "Thank you, President Celente. The people of California Republic are deeply grateful for your assistance. Together, we shall endeavor to rebuild our civilization and support every citizen of California Republic, the greatest place on Earth."

Then the questions from reporters started. Gerald was nowhere to be seen, so I was stuck deflecting serious inquiries about shit I did not know of. Until somebody named Ava rescued me by pretending I had an urgent call from the King of Florida. King of Florida? Fuck that guy. We escaped to the pool area where we found President Celente laughing his ass off. "That was a dirty trick, I told Gerald. What the hell does the President of California do?"

"Fix this shit," Gerald said. "You need to start a breeding program. For the first time in 200 years, California needs more people."

"What the hell is a breeding program?"

"Fucking. Start fucking."

"I never stopped."

"What you need right now are farmers and fuckers."

"Fucking farmers?"

"Precisely. You're quick. You're gonna be the best President of California ever. As long as you keep reading *Trends Journal*."

IN THE NIGHTCLUB, Ava, Dee, and D.D. were leading a conga line all over the dance floor as a couple of women twirled upside-down on poles on the stage. As the President made it rain. Thank God 99% of the world's population is history. A sweaty and out of breath Ava approached as *Get Down Tonight* faded out. "Let's get some air."

Outside, Ava gathered herself, "I didn't think it could get any weirder, Patrick. Make it stop. My head is about to explode."

I almost finished saying, "It's Mr. President," before Ava slapped the shit out of me. And that was enough foreplay for me.

24
PRESIDENT BLACK PATRICK

BRIGHT AND EARLY THE NEXT MORNING, Ava was up, energized, and rattling off the day's schedule. *A schedule? What the fuck is that?*

Gerald's Chief of Staff, Joe Garagiola, was first on the agenda. Joe told me how to structure my team and suggested I interview some of the President's traveling circus, which I did because those meetings were on my packed agenda. Then he told me I needed to put together a plan for my first 100 days, which had already started. And I had a press conference scheduled in 48 hours.

"What's the deal with President? Shouldn't I be a governor?" I asked Joe.

"You're in charge of everything west of the Rockies, north from Cabo San Lucas, south of the North Pole, east of Japan. That means Alaska, British Colombia, Baja, Hawaii, Nevada, Oregon, and Washington. You're taking over North America completely in six months. Gerald needs to concentrate on Europe."

"Damn…"

Joe got up from the table and said, "Gotta go. Breeding appointment."

My next meeting was with one of Gerald's low-level staffers, Alicia. I asked Alicia, "What do you think about repopulating the planet?"

"We need more people, a lot of them, quickly. Before the few remaining intellectuals and scientists die."

"Do we really, though? Do we want another civilization ruled by runaway technology? Do we want first-person shooter games? Cars? Dating apps? Professional sports? The DMV? Cops?"

"You're not the decider, Mr. President. You represent the people. What do the people want? That's what matters."

Well, that bitch isn't getting the job, I decided, as the decider. Next!

I joined Machine Gun and Megan in their cabana.

"We just finished sound check. Your sound system here is amazing," Machine Gun said. "This entire facility is incredible. Can we live here?"

"Yes. Megan, you are Vice President. Machine Gun, you are Minister of Music and Art."

"Deal."

That was easy. Nik and his lovely wife, Nikki, joined us in the cabana. "What jobs do you guys want? You need government jobs."

Nik was put in charge of the military. Nikki assumed the role of Secretary of the Treasury.

Ava, Education. Royce, Fish, Wildlife, Livestock. Xyla, Agriculture.

BLACK PATRICK ALWAYS SAYS, "I'LL TAKE THE ONE ON THE RIGHT."

At our private lunch together, I told Gerald the staff was in place except for a doctor to manage health care and a chief of staff.

"You're meeting with Dr. Doctor later today and Anna after lunch, you're good."

"Dr. Doctor?"

"Yes, Patrick, her legal name is Pamela Doctor. Hire her. And Anna Storm is the smartest human I know, aside from Vice President Napolitano."

"Smarter than Vice President Fox?"

"Bold move, Patrick. Bold move."

"Who's your doctor?" I asked Gerald.

"Dr. Todd Grande."

"Are you fucking kidding me?" I asked Gerald.

"Dr. Drew is too busy. Dr. Phil is too expensive."

"What happened to E.D. Park?" I asked Gerald.

"He's back in Omaha. He's been working for us for a long, long time, Patrick. You, Megan, and Anna are meeting with me and Joe for happy hour, then we're meeting with your full cabinet, then we're having dinner and seeing Machine Gun Kelly."

"Perfect."

"Tomorrow morning we're taking the helicopters to see the smart guys at NASA in Pasadena and hear how fucked we are. Bring your whole crew except Megan, you two can't travel together. On the way back we'll take the scenic route and see how fucked up Los Angeles is, then you can do your TV show."

"Brilliant, Gerald. Brilliant. Let's go ring a bell."

25
THE CABINET

Dr. Doctor, please. I hired Dr. Doctor—she was the only doctor around. The electric Anna Storm? Hired as Chief of Staff—nobody else applied for the job. With our gang of unqualified cabinet and staff in place, we were more than ready to rock. The Top Ten, in no particular order:

Black Patrick, President
Megan Fox, Vice President
Anna Storm, Chief of Staff
Dr. Doctor, Health
Nik Winston, Defense, Logistics, Housing
Nikki Winston, Commerce & Treasury
Ava Avalon, Education
Machine Gun Kelly, Music & Art

Royce Bruno, Fish, Wildlife, Livestock
Xyla Hart, Water, Agriculture, Food

Nik and I met with Gerald's Secretary of Defense, General Hunt, and his staff. Hunt told us there was not much we would ever need to defend—The Last Resort compound was protected by a small detachment of troops guarding the perimeter. Nik's job was all about logistics and delivering necessities—housing and basic services to the people. A team at Edwards Air Force Base was manufacturing modular shipping container homes deliverable by helicopter and assemblage using hand tools. As pockets of survivors were discovered who wanted help Nik would fly in the supplies and personnel needed, and Royce and Xyla would set up food production programs with the people while Ava found smart people to teach people things so civilization could advance again, one day. Hopefully in different directions, this time.

Another major component of Nik's deal was scavenging. Operating factories no longer existed anywhere in the world, so everything, including the kitchen sink, was worth considering for recovery from the rubble. Nik was to arrange for shipping containers to drop in where commodities of value existed, find people to fill them, then retrieve the containers and distribute the goods where needed.

After our meeting, Nik was shaken. "I thought we were running a fucking resort here, not a goddamned planet full of hurricane victims."

"Don't worry, Nik. There are barely any people left. We're dealing with a statewide population the size of Temecula. Without the tourists. I'm the mayor of a small town, you're the guy in charge of the parks. All we do is help people. No cops, no taxes, no bullshit, no assholes. We kill all of the assholes."

"Is that my job, too?"

"Sure, kill 'em all, Nik. Kill 'em all."

At our cabinet meeting before dinner, I saw a roomful of shocked people. Gerald's people had freaked everybody out in individual meetings all day. What had been an unending party at ground zero a few days earlier was now a deadly serious cloud of unending responsibilities and problems swirling overhead.

"This shit is weird as fuck," I said to start the meeting. "Here's how I see the whole thing. President Celente has given us powerful tools to help people who want help. We're not the kind of punishing, fucked-up government we remember—no cops, no laws, no taxes, no bullshit. We find people who want help, we give them everything we possibly can. All we fucking do, all day, every day, is make shit better. Right now people need to learn how to produce their own food and harvest water. And brew beer and distill vodka. If they need help with a home, we can do that instantly. Health care is something we are going to need to figure out real quick. And we need to make sure we're educating the fuck out of anybody who can learn."

"Can you be less specific?" joker Nik asked.

"Good one, Nik. We don't stop having fun. We don't stop partying like motherfuckers. We kill all the assholes."

"We do?" Xyla asked. "We kill people?"

"Yes, we kill assholes. Everybody needs to work together on this planet right now. The good news is, every asshole was a lizard person so we're good."

"What's the definition of an asshole?" Dr. Doctor asked.

"Ava will show you later."

Megan laughed, and everyone else groaned. "Seriously, we will know more after we meet with the team at JPL tomorrow. Their data and information will show us where and how, specifically, we can help people. And, one more thing before the work day ends and happy hour begins," I announced. "I will only serve as President, California Republic, for ten years. That means all of you are only obligated to serve the people of California for ten years, too, so hit the ground running." And then I ran out of the room to the howls of *Ten years?* before somebody could murder me.

Gerald found me in the meditation garden. "That was a very powerful message, Patrick. Where did you come up with that ten years bullshit?"

"The last thing anybody needs in a fucking election or any kind of politics happening anytime soon, if ever. My job is to help people. Everything we could ever need is sitting in a half-demolished Home Depot or Costco somewhere. Food, water, clothing, shelter, health care, education. No fucking bullshit."

"Let's go ring a bell."

Finally, a moment alone with Ava.

"Machine Gun was fucking great, I never knew," Ava said.

"Yeah, his music wasn't bad, either."

Ava punched me and asked, "Why didn't you mention anything about a breeding program today?"

"I'm not talking about that. It's kinda creepy, don't you think? Is this a sex cult? A Nazi people farm?"

"Don't you think we need to encourage people to have kids?"

"Ava, there's no TV, no porn, no TikTok, nothing to do. And there are a lot less fat people. People will be fucking without any encouragement, whatsoever."

"Wow, Patrick, you may be right."

"Do you want to know how you can help?"

"Tell me."

"Go get Megan, the film crew left all of the equipment set up in the chapel. Let's make a movie."

26
HELICOPTERS

Thankfully, Anna found Ava and me in the chapel, shook us awake, dragged us outside, and threw us on a helicopter. "How did you know where to find us?" I asked Anna.

"Everybody knew where you were. There are surveillance cameras everywhere here, Mr. President. We all watched it," Anna responded.

"What was your favorite part?" Ava asked Anna.

"The third hour. Just when we all thought it couldn't get any better, here comes the snowballing."

"Wow. Thank you, Anna." Ava was genuinely flattered by Anna's thoughtful review of her sexual performance. I may have shed a tear, the whole scene was touching.

SO MUCH FOR GETTING ANY MEETING PREPARATION done on the helicopter. Whatever happened in that chapel seemed to reappear in the minds of our whole traveling party every time anybody saw my face. I started to wonder if NASA had access to the chapel camera, too.

"I miss Megan," a hungover Ava moaned.

Gerald and Joe Garagiola were on a separate helicopter. When we hit the ground at JPL they were both, thankfully, all business. "Get on the bus, motherfucker," President Celente said, "this shit's about to get real."

The presentation room was full of scientists, professors, and other people far more intelligent than the late, gray, Neil deGrass Tyson.

The first professor who spoke said, "I want to demonstrate the power of our satellite surveillance equipment. This is a real-time view of the Sylmar Presidential Compound. The professor zoomed in on the chapel and the entire room exploded with laughter, confusing the JPL people. "As you see, we access high-definition visual images leaving little doubt as to the action taking place on the ground." Less explosive laughter, but a lot of chuckles, this time.

The professor handed off the presentation to an analyst (some snickers) who shared details of our shared challenges. "With our aerial assets and artificial intelligence processing we have detected 72,465 people alive in California. We have detected 162 areas of concentration with populations of more than 200 people, the largest of which is 2,600 people in the North Bay area of Northern California. Pasadena/Altadena/San Marino—2,400, The East Bay hills part of the San Francisco Bay Area—1,800, and higher elevations of Studio

City/Beverly Hills—900. Housing, food supplies, and access to water are declining in those areas currently. Please view the data in your packets at the break, we will address any questions at the end of the meeting."

Another professor took the stage and hit us with some knowledge: "Everybody, with maybe a handful of exceptions, within 400 feet of sea level or beneath a dam still alive when the tsunamis hit died. Most people below 800 died in the tsunamis, and many under 1,000 feet died. Everybody on a ship died. 99% of people on airplanes died—the runways were underwater, destroyed, or blocked by flaming wreckage. Billions died in fires, building collapses, sinkholes, leopard attacks—every imaginable way. In the first 90 days after the explosions, hundreds of millions starved to death, hundreds of millions killed others, and millions turned to cannibalism to survive. We have detected a worldwide population of 6.4 million people, with the greatest concentrations being in, surprise, surprise, higher elevation areas such as the Rocky Mountains, South America, Central Europe, Northern Europe, and Appalachia. The population of the United States, including Alaska, is 740,000 people."

Then the real good news came, "The good news about satellites is, they keep working when the whole planet explodes. We've restored 70% of our ground communications, just enough to know what we can expect for Christmas. The planet is smaller. The lizards were here for hundreds of thousands of years hollowing out the inside of our planet. When it all went boom, it all collapsed inward. Additionally, there's no such thing as ice anymore. Antarctica blew up most spectacularly, the North Pole, as well, Greenland is brown now. So, the world is smaller and there's a lot more water. The land mass of Earth has decreased by 44%. It's all gone, for a while. Particulate matter in the atmosphere has dramatically cooled air temperatures worldwide, ocean temperatures will follow, and our models show we are in for some brutal winters for a while. Good news/bad news."

Nik and I knew what we needed to do. We locked ourselves in a conference room, reviewed the data regarding the 162 areas of concentration in California, and selected 50 of immediate significance.

"Professor, I want to see real-time activity in these 50 areas at lunchtime."

"Yes, sir, Mr. President."

Nik said, "Fuck, yeah, let's do this."

An hour later, after another session of doom and gloom, Nik and I hit the situation room at NASA/JPL where walls of video monitors displayed live action all over California. "Can we rewind, we need to see the people?" Nik asked.

Sure enough, we could not only rewind, but we could also tell the AI bot to search for people, children, violence, happy, sad, hungry—if only we'd had this when we ran out of drugs in the past. By the time our lunch break was over, we reviewed all 162 targeted areas plus a dozen more we thought might need help. We arrived at a list of 43 critical, 37 urgent, 52 in need, and 30 who seemed to be functional.

"We get helicopters in the air firing those fucking lawn darts in the ground tomorrow," Nik said.

"Anna, we need the Secretary of Defense."

"Yes sir, Mr. President."

"Mr. Secretary, we've identified communities we need to contact right now. How do you advise we proceed?"

"I don't know."

"What do you mean you don't know?"

"We haven't done that yet."

"What? What the fuck have you guys been doing? With all due respect, sir."

"Killing assholes."

"That makes sense."

Nik said, "Let's drop the first 80 communities a pallet each of paper and markers to communicate to us via their satellites, water, food, a first aid kit, flashlights, a radio, and batteries. A California Republic flag. They can write down what they need, leave notes on roofs, the satellites will tell us what to send, and the next day we send what they need, plus a shortwave radio, solar-powered generator, further instructions."

"You're a fucking genius, Nik. Do it. I need to go see Gerald about a horse."

"GENERAL HUNT, HERE'S A LIST of what we want to be dropped into the first 80 locations, Anna is sending files to be printed. How soon can we get this done?"

    Pallet drop:
        Letter from Not and the President
        Instructions
        Pre-printed pages:
            Do you need help?
                YES/NO
            We urgently need:
                Food
                Water

      Medicine
      Medical Care
      Clothing
      Housing
      Other/Blank pages
      Markers
  California Republic flag
  AM radio & batteries
  Pallet landing zone marking flags
  Flashlights and batteries
  Water
  Food
  First-aid kit

"By 09:00 tomorrow, Mr. President. We have C-17s, C-130s, and Chinooks ready to fly."

"Excellent. Thank you, sir. We need this airlift to continue daily for two weeks minimum, do we have the resources available."

"We have it all, we are waiting for your call. This is the United States of America. There is nothing we cannot do. Think big, President Patrick."

"President Celente, thank you, this has been an invaluable educational experience. We're airdropping supplies into 80 communities in urgent need tomorrow. Eighty more the next day, following up on the initial drops the following day. We will be hitting 160 communities daily, and more, for at least two weeks."

"Your Vice President is at the pool right now. Topless."

"God bless America, Mr. President."

"Nik, we'll be at JPL every other day for the rest of our lives."

"Fuck yeah, we will. I'm staying here for a while. Secretary Hunt and I are organizing a coup."

"Me, too, Our Vice President is topless at the pool right now."

Gerald, Joe, Anna, and I broke the presidential three-helicopter rule and set sail to view potential housing sites and destruction on an enormous scale. None of us said a word as we surveyed the after-effects of what explosions, busted dams, floods, collapsed buildings, roads, and freeways, urban wildfires, and tsunamis, all happening at the same time, did to our friends and family. 98% of the people dead because of some lizard assholes. Then half of the ones who remained died in the subsequent civil unrest, starvation, lack of medical care, shark attacks, and who knows what else. Heartbreaking.

As we came in for a landing in front of the chapel, I told Gerald, "Fuck this first 100 days bullshit. I'm not talking about what I hope to do in 100 days. Fuck that! This is California. We get shit done. I'm talking about my first ten days, motherfucker. Mr. President."

"Yes, you fucking are. Let's go ring a bell."

27
TV SHOW

"GOOD EVENING, PRESIDENT BLACK PATRICK HERE. Today, President Celente, our California Republic staff, and President Celente's staff met with a brilliant group at the Jet Propulsion Laboratory who've been instrumental in helping us identify areas of potential need. Tomorrow morning 80 communities will see helicopter deliveries containing information and tools we want you to use to communicate with us. Wednesday, eighty additional communities will see deliveries, and the first 80 communities will receive supplies based on what you tell us you need. Chief Operating Officer of California Republic, Nik Winston will provide additional details on our communication plan after I finish.

"Do not hesitate to tell us what you need. California is the greatest state in the greatest country on Earth. California Republic is gifted with an abundance of everything we need. It always has been, but now we don't have the assholes here to steal it from us. We will not tolerate assholes, none of us will. We are all in this together.

"California Republic COO Winston will tell you how to communicate with us right now. Please talk to us, we are here to help."

"What the fuck? Do I get a new job every day?"

"Probably. Tell everybody to get in touch with us. This is going to be awesome."

PRESIDENT, CALIFORNIA REPUBLIC: BLACK PATRICK

I went up to the pool, Anna by my side, we sat down at the bar and admired the sunset. And other scenery.

"You sure have had an interesting sixteen hours," Anna said.

"Thank you for helping me with everything, I couldn't have done any of it without you."

"I didn't have anything to do with the chapel ceremony." Anna said, "I know she's a great actress, but she didn't look like she was acting to me."

"What can I do better, professionally? You've been around government people for a while, today's my second day."

"Keep going. You've done more in two days than those Omaha fuckers have done in six months."

"Yikes. Please hit me with unsolicited advice, criticism, whatever, until I become a raging egomaniac."

"You say that now—"

"We're trying to do a lot here, I need help with coherent messaging. I want Californians to know what we're doing, what we're doing next, and what we're doing after that, at all times."

"Go have dinner alone with Ava. Go to sleep early. I'll wake you up at 05:30, we'll have three hours before the fun starts to get that done, among other things."

"I need to see a transcript of Nik's address and a report from NASA first thing. The top priority is finding out what people need and getting it to them if I failed to mention that."

"Eat dinner and go to sleep."

I found Ava, we locked ourselves in our hotel room and ordered a pizza from Rainbow Bar & Grill.

"I'm flying to Reno tomorrow," Ava said, "to loot a remarkably intact textbook warehouse."

"Did the President give you permission to leave California Republic?"

"I'm going to fucking assassinate you…"

28
BRAINDROPS

By 06:00 most of the airdrops scheduled for the day were completed successfully, so we directed Edwards to complete 100 more. Time for lunch.

"Gerald, how did you avoid certain death?"

"Napolitano and I were in my Bell 505 on our way to Roanoke. Your friend, Daniel Tiger, called and asked where I was, I told him I was headed to Roanoke, Virginia to meet with General Hunt, and I was flying a helicopter. He told me he was heading to see his family and didn't know when he'd be back at The Last Resort, but I should visit you in California soon, and you guys were going to be just fine without him. I said I'd ask the General if we could fly his jet into Edwards.

Then he asked, 'So, are you doing that, 'OMAHA-OMAHA-EDWARDS-NINER-ZERO-NINER-OMAHA thing?' I said I was. And that was it."

"Then what happened?"

YOU NEVER KNOW WHAT YOU'RE GONNA GET WHEN DR. SIKORSKY STOPS BY TO SAY HELLO.

"I was on the horn with General Hunt, telling him I was about 30 minutes from the airport when we heard the ear-splitting bang, and the helicopter rose about a thousand feet in altitude. Fire was shooting up into the sky all over the place, the General said, 'Get here quick,' and hung up. I took the Bell up to 12,000 feet and we could see fire everywhere and water flooding everything in every direction. We landed the chopper, jumped in a C-17 with General Hunt, and were airborne in seconds screaming straight up. Three hours later we were sealed inside Cheyenne Mountain where we spent the next ten days."

"Crazy."

"Eighty percent of all operational military aircraft in the United States were airborne when the world went boom. Tankers loaded with fuel, fighters, bombers, transports loaded with troops and cargo, helicopters, everything. All of the Air Force Ones and doomsday planes. The entire political leadership of the country and most of the military brass disappeared."

"Lizards?"

"Lizards. General Hunt was the highest-ranking officer remaining, he met with his team, and they elected me President."

"Insane. Why were so many military aircraft airborne?"

"General Hunt reads *Trends Journal*. And Daniel Tiger got blind drunk one night and told me I didn't know shit about trends, that he was the King of the Lizard People, and he gave me the exact time and date of The Explosion. I told General Hunt. The military had been aware something big was imminent, so Hunt took no chances. Rolled the dice."

GERALD SAVED ALL OF THESE SO HE COULD BE THE C-17 SANTA CLAUS. A FEW HUNDRED C-130S, TOO.

"Nobody will ever believe that story, will they?"

"You're right. After Cheyenne Mountain, Napolitano and I flew to Omaha with Hunt and set up the new government. Because Daniel Tiger suggested Omaha. And then, a few days ago, when you were ready, I flew Air Force One to Edwards, grabbed some choppers, and here we are. Daniel was looking out for us. There's no reason Sylmar should be standing, Edwards should be underwater, along with Omaha, and the tsunamis should have wiped out Roanoke before we blasted off the runway."

"Do you want some mescaline?"

"Yes. I'm off to Cheyenne Mountain. I'll see you in Omaha in 12 days. Get Nik some help, he'll need it."

"Let's go ring a bell."

The next day, President Celente was gone along with his staff. All of the California Republic people were on helicopters, at a military base somewhere, shopping for books, or hanging out with rocket scientists. Anna and I were the only ones at The Last Resort once the Presidential helicopters departed. "Let's get a drink," I told Anna.

Champagne flowed as the 1994 Cabernet from Napa took a breath. Anna said, "Nik needs help before he short circuits. I recommend Machine Gun."

"Machine Gun?"

"Yeah, Machine Gun is no joke. Two or three times a day he pulls me aside and asks all the right questions. He's quietly absorbing everything. Put Vice President Megan in charge of art and music, stick her with Ava."

"I like that idea. As long as Nik is on board."

"Tell him, don't ask him. My glass is empty."

As I refilled Anna's champagne flute, I asked her, "Do you miss Omaha?"

"Fuck no, this place is paradise, you people are a hoot, and we get shit done."

"Your friends and family okay?"

"Yes, the part of Omaha I'm from wasn't wiped out. My small town is even more painfully small, now. I had to get out."

"What are we talking about on our broadcast later?" I asked Anna.

"We did more than we expected today, then spit out some numbers and anecdotes from your staff—they must have seen some amazing things out there today. Then, next, we're doing more, after that we do even more."

I pulled a couple of wine glasses off of the shelf and noticed an envelope with my name on it.

Black Patrick, Open road case number seven. You're welcome, Daniel Tiger. LOL. Lizard Overlord.

"Huh, check this out, Anna. LOL means Lizard Overload? Damn. Do you think we should open road case seven? Maybe it's a bomb."

"Patrick, we are fearless. Let's find out."

Road case number seven was buried under another road case and secured with a padlock. I checked the shelf where the letter was and found the key. Upon opening the lid the contents looked the same as the other road cases filled with cash—bundles of $100 sealed in thick, clear, plastic bags. Underneath a single layer of money bags, we found another box inside with a suitcase-style combination lock. A flashlight beam revealed the code, 420, written on the shelf where the padlock key was discovered. Inside the inside case: a framed, velvet-Elvis-style, portrait of a naked Daniel Tiger petting a leopard. On top of at least 100 pounds of recreational drugs. Powders, pills, liquids, fungi, sheets, and some items neither Anna nor I could identify. We presumed those were suppositories. Anna grabbed four Xanax and four Adderall, shut the lid on the box, and declared, "I'm in charge of this. Here, take these," as she handed me four pills.

"All four?"

"Yes, it's called the Omaha Speedball. Let's move the drug stash into my office and go make pizza for everybody so we can have a decent happy hour today."

We chased our pills with cabernet, wheeled the drug stash into Anna's office hidden in wine boxes so the surveillance cameras wouldn't suspect we were looting the treasury, and hit the kitchen at Rainbow Bar & Grill. As the final pies came out of the oven, helicopters landed and the whole gang hit the rooftop, poolside bar for our traditional happy hour soiree.

"Welcome back, everyone! Grab a drink, some pizza, shots, whatever. I need five minutes with each of you so I can give the people of California Republic their evening dose of information. Xyla, you're first, next is Machine Gun."

Xyla observed suitable locations for greenhouses and food forests in every community her helicopter flew over. I chose Xyla first to give her time to prepare remarks for her address to the people after mine. Next was Machine Gun, who gave very specific information in a concise, effective manner. He said we were doing exactly the right thing, but we needed to do much more. I told him to tell Nik what he saw. Ava delivered tons of books to Edwards and swore she saw a rave happening on the shores of Lake Tahoe. Dr. Doctor said people needed insulin ungently, Royce saw giraffes, kangaroos, and monkeys running around in the Sierras. Nik was last, he looked fried. "You need help, Nik."

"No shit, Machine Gun."

"That was easy." We called Machine Gun over and told him he was now handling logistics and heading to JPL with Nik the next day. "Fuck yeah. I'm all in."

"Machine Gun, do you want to speak to the people after my radio address tonight?"

"Absolutely."

Nik reported, "We dropped 280 emergency aid pallets today. Far more than the 80 we expected to deliver. Some communities were obviously in need of more than one pallet, so we gave them more. We discovered new populations as people heard helicopters in the skies—it seems there are more people in bunkers and basements than we imagined. Four C-17s dropped substantial amounts of food and water on the largest twelve communities. We have a list via NASA's satellites of urgent needs. People need a lot of everything, mostly food. We discovered an intact Costco store in Manteca guarded by two, fiercely-loyal Costco employees. Those two are loading helicopters with goods as we speak. They'll be arriving here in the morning with the helicopters from Edwards. I suggest we hire them—we need help around here.

"Tomorrow: we deliver everything we can which is everything we have been asked for, so far. Plus generators, shortwave transceivers, and lots of food.

"Next, after that, we continue to fulfill requested items, and we deliver the first batch of food production supplies."

"Excellent," I responded. "Identify one of those satellite geniuses at JPL you want to work here on-site."

"I already have, Chester's here along with the NASA IT guys tomorrow morning," Nik said. "We don't need to go to JPL, JPL is coming to us."

"Unbelievable. We dropped AM radios today, right?"

"Hundreds."

"Perfect. Do we need to go write a speech, Anna?"

"Nope, here it is," Anna said as she handed me three sheets of paper. "Ad lib the ending part about California Republic's abundance after the part about executing assholes."

"That's not, not half-bad. We all need champagne, time for a toast."

29
DAY FOUR

MORNING REPORT: HUNDREDS OF MESSAGES OF GRATITUDE, California Republic loves Xyla and Machine Gun. C-17s and Chinooks delivered goods with tremendous efficiency. Many communities received two or more separate deliveries as requests were filled within hours, in some cases.

Agriculture savant Xyla and animal guy Royce flew off in separate helicopters to observe pallet drops and survey the scene from above. Our evolving staff roster:

Black Patrick, President
Megan Fox, Vice President, Arts
Anna Storm, Chief of Staff
Dr. Pamela Doctor, Health

Nik Winston, Chief Operating Officer
Nikki Winston, Commerce & Treasury
Ava Avalon, Education
Machine Gun Kelly, Logistics
Royce Bruno, Fish, Wildlife, Livestock
Xyla Hart, Agriculture
Dee, Resort Operations
D.D., Resort Operations
Chester, JPL

Nik and Machine Gun set up the artificially intelligent satellite communications war room with Chester and the IT crew from JPL while Vice President Fox, Ava, Nikki, and Dr. Doctor learned how to operate a shortwave and prepared for a full day of fun hearing from the people.

Anna and I met with Costco Manteca heroes Steve and Doug, who would be our honored guests, along with Chester from JPL, at the mandatory happy hour meeting.

I asked the Costco duo, "How did you guys survive the floods and save the store?"

"The carbon monoxide detectors and fire alarms in the store went off so everybody ran out of the building and all the way down the hill to the street," Doug related. "We were on the roof smoking hash so we were the only ones left. The Explosion knocked us down, walls of fire were everywhere—"

"Our gas station blew up," Steve said.

Doug continues, "Then we saw water closing in from every direction. We ran down the ladder off the roof, closed all the roll-up doors, duct-taped and spray-foamed around all of the edges, threw down towels, pillows, mattress toppers, and dog beds—we did everything we could to try to stop the water we saw coming."

Steve added, "The power went out, but our backup generator kicked in, so we unboxed every shop vac and fan we could find and pointed them at the doors."

"The water slammed into the building about ten feet high on all sides at once," Doug said. "The tire shop doors were all fucked-up so a lot of water came in through there and fucked up the optometry section."

"The water went away but then it came back harder the second time, then maybe five feet high the third time," Steven said.

"Wow, amazing. What did you do after that?"

"We cracked some beers and had a barbecue," Doug answered.

"For nine months?"

"Pretty much."

"We wiped out the Vicodin in the pharmacy, too," Steve boasted.

"Are you hiring?" Doug asked.

"Maybe, what do you guys do?"

Turns out they both worked in the Costco food court. We hired Steve and Doug to run the food and beverage operation at The Last Resort effective immediately, showed them the kitchen, and instructed them to prepare a buffet lunch for 20, ready in three hours, no pizza.

"Anything else on the schedule today before happy hour?" I asked Anna.

"15:00 call with President Celente."

"Perfect. I want to present Steve and Doug with Presidential Medals at Happy Hour. Do we have anything around here we can use for a medal temporarily?"

"There's a box of Insane Clown Posse jewelry backstage at the amphitheater."

"Outstanding, let's go talk to some people on shortwave."

All of the gear was installed and functioning in the war room. Chester automated visual requests from satellite imagery to transmit to Edwards after approval from Machine Gun. Transcribed shortwave conversations were treated the same way. Dr. Doctor's morning wasn't going well. "We've medevac'd three patients in the past two hours."

"We start with medics on the ground in two weeks. Do we need to accelerate that?"

"Let's see how the day goes."

"Your call."

"Chester, amazing work. Can AI detect who the intelligent people are by the satellite images and shortwave conversation?"

"With 100% accuracy."

"Assholes?"

"Same deal. In real time."

"I need a 1-page report of who and where the smart people are, and the supporting information AI uses to make that determination at 16:00."

"Anna, what time is the Omaha thing today?" I asked with a wink.

"Five minutes, Mr. President. In the Situation Room."

The mid-morning Kentucky bourbon/Omaha Speedball combination is one of life's great pleasures.

"Vice President Napolitano will be here tomorrow morning, leaving the following afternoon," Anna said.

"Beautiful."

"I'm sending a pot of coffee and Ava to your suite. You need to spend time with her. Sit in the sun on the balcony and say nice things. And listen to her. Don't talk about yourself. Period. Mr. President."

"Am I doing something wrong?"

"No. It's my job to make sure you never, ever, do."

Ava and I sat on the balcony outside our room in the warm sunshine and admired the rewilding taking place on the cemetery grounds. Since most of the planet was a burial ground now, our compound for dead people was obsolete and Xyla's planting posse had taken it over.

"We need to form a band," Ava said. "This place needs rock 'n' roll again."

"That's a great idea."

I MET WITH NIK AND MACHINE GUN for lunch. "Nik, Gerald wants us in Omaha now. Vice President Napolitano is spending the day with us here tomorrow then, I have a feeling, we're off to Nebraska. Machine Gun, we'll be around if you need anything, but I doubt you will."

"He's ready," Nik said.

"Gerald's going to want us to start sending him help right away. We need capable people here right now. Ava will contact and interview intelligent citizens, based on the AI assessment, every day, and get them in here for education on water harvesting and food production with Xyla. Ava will also determine who we want to keep here to help out—we can't all be working at a telephone help desk every day."

Machine Gun reported, "We delivered more than 400 pallets today, including 122 same-day requests. We continue to find pockets of survivors as yet undiscovered due to helicopter and airplane noise. We're sending a couple of fighter jets up and down all parts of the state still above water to see if we can find more."

"Any shortwave issues?"

"None," Nik said. "We learned today the shortwave transceivers are actually satellite telephones programmed to only dial one number."

"Perfect. Need anything?"

"No, we're good. Tomorrow is more food, requested items, and horticulture supplies and equipment. Saturday we start dropping shipping container houses."

The daily call with President Celente was brief. Gerald spent most of the call ranting about that little fuck, Macron. The happy hour and dinner festivities and meetings ended the day with a bang. Xyla was excited about working with future farmers and humbled by her newfound celebrity as a result of her radio appearance, Ava was ready to handle the closing act on this evening's broadcast, Vice President Fox couldn't wait to deliver her first in a series of solo Saturday Night Live broadcasts in my stead. Dr. Doctor reported the six patients evacuated by helicopter were doing well at Edwards.

Anna slipped me a couple of ICP medallions and framed certificates then banged on a wine glass and said I had an announcement to make.

"California Republic is the greatest place on Earth. We are the best. We are the best survivors, that's for sure. When I see a champion in action, I make sure we all recognize the champion's outstanding actions. Two men are here with us today who are responsible for the food thousands of hungry Californians are eating right now. Right fucking now! Steve and Doug saved an entire Costco store's food, clothing, pharmaceuticals, and so much more, from The Explosion and tsunami that wiped out their entire community. And then they guarded that Costco like hawks! For months! Until yesterday! When Nik and Machine Gun sent in a team and brought them to us. On behalf of the people of California Republic, from the desert to the mountains to the sea, Steve and Doug, I present you both with the Hero of California Republic Presidential Medal."

Anna said, "That was beautiful. Nice work."

"Thank you, Chief. After dinner, I'm calling some of the people who called in today. You're welcome to join me, but tomorrow will be a really long day."

"I'll see you at 06:00."

Over dinner, I told Ava I needed her to recruit smart people and bring them to The Last Resort for training with Xyla, she loved the idea. Nikki told me she loved speaking with people on the radios, I invited her to share her experience with the people to close the radio show, she was thrilled. During the show I said I would be calling as many people as I could around the state for a couple of hours after the show. That was the plan, at least.

30
OMAHA

Vice President Napolitano arrived bright and early and joined our 08:00 morning meeting. He listened intently, posed prescient questions, and impressed the California Republic crew. At the conclusion, Vice President Napolitano told Nik and I, "That was remarkable information. I need you two in Omaha right now."

I looked at Nik, he was ready. Anna needed ten minutes. I asked the Vice President, "Would you mind taking Vice President Fox aside and giving her some pointers, how a Vice President handles the absence of the President?"

"Twist my arm."

As one Vice President scurried away to advise another Vice President, Nik said, "You did that just to fuck with him."

"Let's go ring a bell."

Fortified with cocaethylene, reposado, and Anna's pill recipe du jour, the four of us screamed across the country in Napolitano's Gulfstream and arrived early for lunch in Omaha. "Are we poor?" I asked Gerald.

"No, we don't need money anymore."

"Then why is our nation's capital such a pile of shit?"

"Why I outta. Not every capital is a five-star California resort."

"That's right, every capital is, except yours."

"Listen you little—" And that was the first time a president put me in a chokehold. All in good fun.

Napolitano told Gerald what he had seen and heard in our morning meeting. Gerald said, "You guys are taking this shit to a whole 'nother level every fucking day!"

"Yes, we fucking are. You're looking at champions in action. We never stop challenging ourselves. We're always looking for ways we can do more and better."

Nik gave President Celente all the advice he needed: "You need a JPL guy and a Machine Gun Kelly here right now." Gerald agreed, Joe Garagiola called JPL, NASA sent a guy over to The Last Resort to hang with Chester for a couple of hours, then they put Omaha's new NASA/JPL guy in the back seat of an F-15EX. Omaha's JPL guy would arrive that very evening.

"I need to do my radio show at 17:00 and I'd like you two to join me," I told Celente and Napolitano. "I was on the phone with Californians all over the state until 3 a.m. last night and they have questions."

In unison, Anna and Nik—"You were?"

"It was awesome. Every single person I called had listened to the radio show that evening. Every single person expressed gratitude for our help and sounded excited about the future."

Gerald lit up like a Christmas tree and told Joe, "Get Hunt, find our Machine Gun Kelly, then lock Nik and our MGK clone in a room together, and don't let 'em out. After lunch. Let's go ring a bell."

Lunch was served in Gerald's glass cube on the rooftop of the United States Capitol building—a converted Airport Sheraton. "Joe, what are those fuckers doing over there in Cheyenne Mountain?" Gerald asked his Chief of Staff.

"As far as I can tell, they spend most of their time looking for zebras running around in what's left of Canada."

"We don't have any external or internal threats to worry about anymore. Let's get 'em outta that cave and reacquaint 'em with civilization. I had a briefing with NASA this morning. Water's receding in many places—soaking into the soil, filling in the blanks where the lizards left tunnels intact."

"In California, we're finding out there are a lot more people than NASA previously detected. In places we thought were devoid of human life," Nik said. "When helicopters or airplanes fly over areas for the first time in a year or so, people crawl out of their holes and wave."

"Joe, I want jets and helicopters flying over every county in the country that isn't underwater when the sun comes up tomorrow."

Nik continued, "All the plane or chopper has to do is make noise to get people outside, the satellites and computers do the geolocation and population count."

"Did any of the Goodyear blimps survive?" I wondered aloud.

THE ENEMY OF HUMAN CIVILIZATION, OCCUPIED BY LIZARD PEOPLE. BANNED IN CALIFORNIA REPUBLIC.

"Gerald, we need boots on the ground in California, "I told the President. "We'll consider anyone in Cheyenne Mountain who wants out of that place. We're not running a government out there, we're helping people. We send people what they tell us they need and we spread good news. No taxes, no bills, no cops, no money, no bullshit. We only have one chance to do this right. This is serious shit and the most fun any of us have ever had."

"You're going to need to handle a few more states out there," Gerald said.

"No, I'm not. Fuck that. Nevada Nik. Machine Gun Montana. Steve Arizona. We'll develop the talent and send them off to succeed, but I'm not doing shit in those hillbilly hellholes outside of California."

"Who's Steve?"

"Show him the picture, Anna."

"What the fuck?"

"We found Steve and Doug Wednesday. Helicopters flew over Northern California and saw an SOS sign made out of pool noodles floating in the water."

Nik elaborated, "Steve and Doug saved an entire Costco store from the floods and guarded it for months. Yesterday we presented them both with the Hero of California Republic Presidential Medal. While we were giving 'em their awards, thousands of hungry Californians were eating the food Steve and Doug protected in that Costco. People are hungry out there, Mr. President. Every community is demanding food deliveries and we are giving the people what they need."

Anna said, "Ava found five people last night to train immediately to grow food, we picked them up this morning. As we speak, Xyla is working with them at The Last Resort."

"We haven't even been doing this shit a week. People are fucking hungry. There is no time to waste. We're in Omaha for 48 hours, max, then we need to leave for California. If you want our help in the Rockies, Appalachia, or anywhere else, give us about ten days and send the Gulfstream or three F-15s."

"I don't have to tell you we are making history here," President Celente said.

"We're just helping people help people. You saved us all. And nobody will ever believe your story. I do. I know it's true. You get the statues."

"What story?" Anna and Nik asked, in unison, again.

"Let's get civilization back on its feet first and then we'll tell you the *Tale of the Tiger*."

GERALD INVITED NIK, ANNA, AND I TO GO FOR A WALK AROUND OMAHA. What's that? A walk? We never left our compound in Sylmar unless we were in an armored helicopter. "Places like Omaha, Denver, and Colorado Springs, still function as if the cataclysm never happened, to some extent," Gerald explained. "People still use money, go to work at bullshit jobs, some still drive cars, watch team sports, belong to political parties, go to church—"

Nik and I looked at each other in disbelief. "I don't think we can help you fix this kind of bullshit," I told Gerald. "You've got your work cut out for you. You can never help these people make themselves happy."

"I've heard enough," Nik said. "This is hell on Earth."

"Where are the lizards when you need 'em?" I asked no one in particular.

"I refuse to help these people," Nik declared. "Was that a cop?"

"Yes, we still have a few cops here..."

"These are people pretending to be people," Nik observed.

I told Gerald, "If you want us to grant you political asylum in California Republic, let me know."

"We still get the *Wall Shit Journal* here," Gerald said, with that man on death row walking to the gas chamber look in his eyes.

"Brutal. We need tequila."

While Gerald went to walk the dog, I told a wise man, "Nik, we have to secede from the United States."

"How?"

"We show the people of California Republic how different we are. As soon as we get back home, we spend every minute of every day helping our people in every way possible, in the kindest way possible."

"We're already doing that."

"Tell Chester I need the transcripts of all of the calls from today. I'm calling every single Californian who reached out for help today after we're done with dinner if it takes all night. And I'm axing Celente and Napolitano from the radio show tonight."

"How?"

"I'm doing the usual update, then I'm interviewing Steve and Doug. The people demand we share the story of Steve, Doug, and the battle of Costco Manteca. And that will go on for a long time until Anna says we're out of time."

"That'll work."

"California Republic is its own planet. It never needed to belong to America. We gotta get out. Don't tell anyone, they'll execute us both."

"Tell anyone what?" Anna asked.

"Omaha hookers," Nik said.

"There's a strip joint around the corner that's open until 4 a.m.," Anna said. "Full bar, all nude."

"We can't go, I'm making phone calls all night."

"I'll handle the phone calls tonight. Say hi to my identical twin at Whompin' Gazongas."

"We have three hours until the radio show," I told Nik.

"Two hours. Let's wait until after dinner."

The radio show went off without a hitch. MGK and crew delivered more than 500 pallets of food and other aid, the helicopter heroes evacuated five more patients in need of medical care, pop-up greenhouse kits and supplies to grow food arrived, Ava identified six new students to add to Xyla's survival courses—the sound of California Republic roaring back to life was deafening.

Steve and Doug stole the show with their inspirational tale of being in the right place at the right time—smoking hash on the roof of a Costco. President Celente and Vice President Napolitano said hello to California Republic. Dinner with the Federal government reinforced the instinctual fight-or-flight within Nik and I. Anna gave us each a stack of cash, a handful of pharmaceutical products, and sent us off to explore Nebraska. Like champions.

I was all things anti-Omaha until my eyes readjusted to the darkness inside Whompin' Gazongas. Stalking the shadows a creature lit in black light in a skin-tight crimson leotard, with long yellow fingernails, yellow fangs for teeth, sharp yellow horns growing out of her head through tousled jet-black hair and a pointy tail protruding from someplace within her evilness who spotted fresh meat. She was hungry. I temporarily sacrificed Nik to the evil one and began double-fisting beverages at the bar. Somehow the devilish Anna look-a-like charmed her way into the California Republic posse. What happens on the road, stays on the road, Ava.

President Celente sensed our disappointment with the prospects for any type of radical shift in middle America's appreciation for all things human. As Gerald waved goodbye and our California Republic crew rode to the airport in an old-fashioned vehicle known as an automobile, Anna handed out the pills. New recruit Lana celebrated by biting my leg. As the gate opened and we sped onto the tarmac Nik asked, "Where's the Gulfstream?" The driver made a sharp turn into an airplane hangar where we were ushered into an office and outfitted in flight suits. Then came the helmets with elephant trunk-like hoses. And then we were led out the other side of the hangar where four F-15s awaited. Up the ladder, into the rear seat, back in California in less than an hour.

Two seats, two engines, coast-to-coast in under two hours. F-15EX

"On the ground at Edwards Air Force Base, soon to be known as Fort Celente if I have anything to do with it, I asked Anna, "Did that just happen?"

"It's still happening to Lana, Anna said. "Anything makes her orgas—"

"Xyla!"

On the way to the helipad from the F-15s, we saw the one and only Xyla waving at a pair of helicopters lifting off and away. Xyla joined the Omaha crew and we all boarded a Blackhawk and sped off into the sunset. Xyla looked emotionally and physically demolished—she had been at Edwards sending her first batch of eight graduates home to apply their new-found farming knowledge in the wild. She was also pissed. "All fucking day, every fucking day, we get messages from parents telling us their children are starving. In California. Starving! In California! We need to do more!"

"We've delivered more than 10,000 tons of aid in our first week. That's more than 200 pounds per person. Half of that, at least, was food. We're going to double that this week and double it again next week. Nik, we need to go see some people on the ground tomorrow morning. Xyla, where do you advise we go first?"

CALIFORNIA REPUBLIC SHIPPING CONTAINER HOUSE.
ALSO KNOWN AS THE STABBIN' CABIN.

"Let's review the data back home," Xyla said. Before she asked, "Why are there two Annas now?"

Lana said, "Because they couldn't find another Xyla."

"Holy shit!" Nik exclaimed. "We'll be back in time for happy hour!"

Time travel via an airplane flying faster than the Earth spins into an earlier time zone is the best. As the magnificence of The Last Resort came into view whatever ill will I felt in Omaha vanished. We landed, headed for happy hour, and caught up with the posse, which had grown by three with the addition of a trio of bright Californians Ava brought in from the wilderness to staff the help desk. Royce found an operational fish farm in Central California, so he was helicopter-dropping fish into ponds and lakes where locals had asked for them and re-stocking The Last Resort's ponds. Xyla, with her new sidekick, Lana, in tow, brought me a list of places where children were starving and said, "Here, they're expecting you tomorrow morning. The chopper's here at 05:00."

MGK and Nik reviewed the past couple of days' progress with Chester and worked themselves up into a frenzy of productivity. Dr. Doctor was in touch with healthcare providers all over the state and together they were developing a system to deliver necessary services. Nikki was guarding the state treasury like a champion, Steve and Doug were loving their new celebrity and wore their ICP medals 24/7, and Dee and D.D. kept the wheels from falling off.

"You need to prepare your radio show," party-pooper Anna said as she handed me a gel cap the likes of which I had never seen.

"We need to be on a helicopter at 05:00. Weaverville, Burney, Baxter, Wawona, and Poker Flat."

"Did you poke 'er flat last night?" Anna asked.

"Poker in the front, liquor in the rear," Ava said as she sat down on the President's lap. "Why don't you let me host the show tonight? Sixty Minutes with Ava. Every Sunday night."

"Yes."

With most of my work done for the day, I found Vice President Fox. She said, "Let's go ring a bell."

I told Megan, "I heard your show last night, we listened to it with the President."

"Was he happy?"

"No! He was pissed. 'Why don't I have a Megan? Why don't I have a Nik? Why don't I have a Machine Gun, I want to shoot myself!'"

"What about my cousin?"

"We never saw her. I'm calling a dozen or so Californians later, would you like to join me?"

"Sure. I'll call, too, until the first person I call asks, 'What are you wearing?' So that means I'll make one phone call."

"Are you offended people objectify you?"

"The day I'm not objectified will be the worst day of my life."

"I've not heard that perspective before."

"Objectification is an art, like everything else. Everybody can paint, few can do it masterfully."

"Word."

31
WEEK TWO

OUR FIRST STOP ON THE STARVING CHILDREN TOUR was a dusty, hellhole of a trailer park in the middle of what once was Yosemite National Park—Wawona, California. The tribe's leader, a 400-pound beast of a woman wearing a *Roll Tide* T-shirt, was a real battle-axe. "My kids is starvin' We need food."

The clump of overall-wearing, filthy children looked up from their whitlin' and said, "We's starvin'."

Nik said, "Tell me what you need. You'll have it today," as I observed a man in a rickety shed using parts and pieces of the greenhouse kit we delivered to them as components for a drug lab, allegedly.

"I need ten pepperoni pizzas, two dozen chocolate cupcakes, and a six-pack of Diet Coke—the big bottles, two liters. It's my baby daddy's sister's half-sister's birthday today."

Nik arranged for the requested birthday supplies and a chunk of Costco Manteca's Lunchables supply to land in Wawona later that day.

"There's no way to help those people," I told Nik.

"Should we turn off their shortwave and tell NASA to blur Wawona on their maps so we don't ever have to think about this place again?"

"We have to. For the survival of the human race."

"But, the kids is starvin'."

"That's the least of their problems. Inbreeding is not just a lifestyle in Wawona."

Flying low and slow over the Sierras, Nik and I couldn't help wondering how many Unabombers were living large hunting all of the pandas and koalas now native to California Republic. We took incoming fire a few times, no big deal. By the time we returned to The Last Resort, Nik, Anna, and I were suicidal. Everything we saw was depressing. Discouraging. Except for that herd of hippos murdering a guy who looked like the vocalist in Coldplay That was amazing.

At happy hour, Nik and I regrouped. Nik was confused. "What do we do? Everybody who survived is a fucking moron."

"Death squads. And let's get a list from Ava of smart people and visit them tomorrow."

The "smart" people we visited the next day should have been killed in The Explosion, so we wouldn't have to.

"Drop grass-fed, and grass-finished, or drop nothing at all! We are not savages here on the hill."

"Your helicopters disturb my swans."

"Bring a hairstylist next time."

"Since you took over, California has gone downhill. We never had problems like this with the TV before! I'm moving to Florida. Kiss my ass!"

"Anna, I want to marry your sister. And Ava. What do you think?"

"Do it. Then start a band. Black Patrick and the First Ladies."

"I like that idea. A power trio. Any other ideas?"

"Lana dreams about you snorting cocaine out of her belly button."

"That's not an idea. That's a fantasy I've implanted in her brain."

"Not really. She saw the video of you, Ava, and Megan in the chapel."

"How come I've never seen that video?"

"Because you're not invited. While you're doing your radio show every Monday, the rest of us are watching that video on the big screen in the amphitheater."

"Even Ava?"

"Especially Ava. Her play-by-play is hilarious. Megan gives the color commentary. It's a little bit different every time."

"I'm not sure how I feel about that."

"Megan makes all of the new people take notes. And then she reads the funny ones the next week."

"Sounds like it's time to make a sequel, with your sister, this time."

"I'll put it on your schedule."

And then I woke up.

"Nik, there's only one way to fix this whole deal or blow it all up. It's time to tell the *Tale of the Tiger*."

"We can't. Even if we hate 'em 'cause we ain't 'em. Remember the California Republic motto?"

"Fuck."

"California Republic: Always do the Right Thing."

32
TALE OF THE TIGER

DANIEL TIGER WAS NEVER BORN, THEREFORE, HE CAN NEVER DIE. One guy, in a shiny tie, living a lie, behind evil eyes.

You remember Daniel Tiger from infomercials on a device known as a television. Daniel sold so much shampoo he controlled the port of Fiji and insisted the pronunciation of Fiji was Fee-GEE, not FEE-gee. That's why he's never had any friends. Since his series of mild mini-strokes, Daniel Tiger has come to appreciate the healing powers of coconut water and Epsom salts. Nobody knows where Daniel Tiger learned how to elicit hatred in those within his orbit. Except me.

In a dream state, Daniel Tiger appeared. "Open the door!" Daniel Tiger yelled at me from the other side of our shared bistro table on the rooftop patio.

"Which door? The door that leads to Jupiter, or Neptune, or Uranu—"

"Silence! I know the fucking planets. Open the door to your mind."

"Did you know, Costcos never have windows?"

When I met Daniel Tiger, I heard what he said, but didn't quite grasp the seriousness of his message. My days were consumed writing terrible reggae-like music to accompany his witty lyrics about zoo animals, such as *Monkey Needs a Banana*.

Monkey needs a banana

Put your number
Into my phone
The smile on your face
Nobody's home
I'm real
You can trust me
As far
As a blind tiger can see

Monkey see a banana
Monkey needs a banana

Number one
Baby it's you and me
You take the cake
In my menagerie
Help this blind man see I need to believe

Make me a sandwich
Or get up and leave

Monkey see a banana
Monkey needs a banana

Trends Journal predicted an imminent uptick in animal attacks. Armed with this information, as President of California Republic, my duty to help the people avoid wild animal encounters and the resulting horrible injury and death compelled immediate action.

"Royce, did we ever talk about your job responsibilities?"

"No," Royce answered. "You said we don't do that in California Republic."

"True. Most of the time. You're responsible for every animal in California Republic."

"That's not much responsibility at all. I ran the produce department at Whole Foods when my boss went on vacation."

"We know, thanks for telling that story again. Anyway, why do we have gorillas and Komodo dragons in California now?"

"Locally, animals escaped from zoos. Globally, wild animals unhappy with economic conditions elsewhere, say, Africa and Southeast Asia, rode tsunamis here to start over in California Republic, the land of opportunity, where the streets have no names."

"Motherfucker, I want two of whatever you're snorting, you must be on some great shit. How do you explain the elephant owls? The pelican gophers? The doo-wop wolves?"

"Daniel Tiger."

"He was a Daniel and a tiger?"

"No. He was cross-breeding wild animals when he wasn't cross-dressing."

"He was fucking animals in negligees?"

"Yes, but he was also cross-breeding polar bears with kangaroos, porcupines with eagles, crazy shit like that."

"How do you know this shit?"

"I own a banjo."

Daniel Tiger couldn't bring his lizard self to kill his beloved animals on his way off this planet, but he didn't mind killing nine billion people. Can't say I disagree. I have only one problem with Daniel's exit strategy—Why did he have to leave his pets behind? That's just wrong, Michael Jackson.

Royce said, "There's this one ostrich I saw on the satellite south of Fresno. It looked like Taylor Swift."

"So, it looked like Taylor Swift? Did it sound like shit?"

"Yeah."

"The ostrich was Taylor Swift, then. Basic powers of deduction."

"It can't be Taylor Swift. All the lizards went away."

I had to admit, Royce knew what he was talking about. "You're right, but, where the fuck is E.D. Park?"

"Vegas."

"Fuck, I hope he's not there with that guy from Iceland, again."

"He is. And your friend who runs the Thai mafia, too. That Pomeranian of his has eaten the face off at least a hundred passed-out hookers."

"Whatever happens in Vegas, means nothing to us. We are California Republic. FUCK everyone else."

"They hate us 'cause they ain't us."

What I failed to take away from my conversation with animal guy Royce hit me like a hammer in the middle of a sex dream about fucking my own Vice President in the greenhouse again —Mikayla was still alive and running his organized crime business near the border of California Republic. In most cases, masses of potentially hostile neighbors—resentful Oregonians, sun-baked Arizonans—were easily dismissed. What were they going to do, climb over mountains or hike across deserts to steal California Republic's bountiful treasure? However, Mikayla owned a warehouse full of military-grade all-terrain vehicles and commanded an army of Muay Thai fighters fired up on crystal meth ready for battle at the drop of a ngob.

"President Celente, who's in charge of Nevadia?"

"The King of Thailand, as far as I can tell."

"That's not good. Doesn't that guy have an army of sex soldiers who fly fighter jets?"

"Yes. They were all at Nellis working on their bombing skills when the planet imploded. Somehow, Nevada is 60% Thai now,"

"Are you concerned we might be dealing with leftovers there?"

"No. They're not evil enough. Total weirdos, but no threat to human civilization," Gerald reported. "In other news, we found a warehouse full of guitars in Indiana yesterday. Fort Wayne. I'm told the place was the size of a dozen Costcos."

"How did a place that close to all of the Great Lakes survive?"

"It didn't. Everything in the warehouse was destroyed except the stock on the shelves above the 20-foot level. Do you want it? We don't know what to do with it."

"Yes. Vice President Fox and Ava will spread it around. They're really good at that."

"Send video."

"By the way, we found an Iron Mountain facility in Shasta Mountain with a treasure trove of pre-explosion American film, music, literature, art, and who-knows-what-else. We're not touching anything in there anytime soon. That reminds me, did the doomsday seed vault survive?"

"We don't think so. Svalbard is still underwater. Every place that once was an island is still underwater."

"Even Australia?"

"Australia is a continent, you moron."

AVA WAS GETTING RESTLESS. "We gotta get out of here or we'll die, spiritually. The intermingling of people and ideas is the only way people grow and evolve in any meaningful way. We've created a great little refuge here and populated it with the kind of wackos we want to hang out with. As if we are some kind of gatekeepers of what's cool."

I agreed with Ava. "Everybody still alive any of us have ever met who's wanted to move here lives here. Except the missing person nobody's missing formerly known as Steven Seagal."

"You're right. How do we encourage the people of California Republic to express themselves? Create? Wop bopabula?"

"FLSD," I responded.

"What's that?"

"Friday LSD."

After the first three weeks of daily or more deliveries of urgently needed supplies, we transitioned to a weekly delivery schedule where orders were collected all week and fulfilled on Fridays.

Vice President Fox was all-in on the FLSD concept and announced she would participate live in the inaugural *Friday LSD* event and, most likely, on her *Saturday Night Live* show, as well. She instructed interested communities to place LSD signage on rooftops for the satellites and, just to be safe, contact her, personally, via shortwave, to ensure their Friday LSD order was in our system. Well, we discovered everybody wanted to fry on acid with Vice President Fox, which was awesome. We also learned our LSD wasn't as good as most of the LSD being manufactured in Northern California. Anyway, we dropped pallets of supplies, including LSD, on Friday.

Edwards was running out of warehouse space, so we included a lot of weird shit for people to play with while tripping in acid—Halloween costumes, percussion instruments, fog machines, inflatable furniture, wigs, air raid sirens, and whatever else we needed to get rid of.

All of the FLSD party packages arrived by 10:00 and the entire population of California Republic finished their In-N-Out burgers, passed out for a few, and awakened to the sound of bugles at 14:00 signaling the time to place a little piece of paper with a strikingly-realistic illustration of a Vice President's body embossed upon it onto their tongues and leave it there until instructed otherwise by the Vice President.

At 15:00 AM radios all over California Republic crackled back to life followed by the Vice President saying, "Meow. Meow? Meow!" in every Yoko Ono language for 20 minutes while MGK fucked with a theremin and the rest of us made psychedelic bell music. Somebody built a slip-n-slide. One of us randomly operated a klaxon horn for the next 12 hours. Royce figured out how to play records backward. Ava and I retreated to our home and went to sleep, eventually.

The next morning, we air-dropped every community in California Republic a double dose of LSD and more weird shit. They say LSD doesn't work two days in a row. That's true, unless you double the dose.

33
FLYING MACHINES

"Chester, who's the smartest scientist at JPL?" I asked the smartest scientist I knew.

"Me."

"Perfect, here's your new job. We need 25,000 flying machines. Remember cars?"

"Vaguely."

"We need 25,000 flying machines we can deliver to our California Republic posse in three weeks. Whatever it takes."

"Consider it done. I'll be at Edwards in case of emergency."

Chester left us for a couple of weeks then appeared silently and unexpectedly in the skies above The Last Resort during our ritual happy hour one day. Floating, maneuvering, flying on a magical machine. As he slowly folded his kite-like contraption's wings together, Chester descended from above and splashed down in the pool next to a naked former stripper from Omaha.

"It works! We're building 30,000 of these at Edwards right now."

"What is it?"

"It's a solar-powered ultralight made out of rope, guitar strings, and yoga pants."

"You stole the idea from the contents of my nightstand?"

"Yes. It runs on two triple-A batteries, too."

"That's not very nice. How do you make it go faster?"

"Slap it."

"How does it turn?"

"Pull its hair."

"How far does it go?"

"All the way. It's crash-proof, it folds up like an umbrella, anybody can fly it, like a champion, and it hauls a thousand pounds of ass."

"That's almost four Oprahs. It sounds like magic."

"Every motherfucking thing we do is magic or we don't do it," Chester said. Chester said. Bam!

Every nook and cranny of California Republic received California Republic Flyers and, instantly, Californians were connected, once again. So we decided to invite everybody to The Last Resort for a barbecue. Everybody. The entire population.

"President Celente, we need you, man. We're having a barbecue and you're the guest of honor."

"What's the occasion?"

"We invented a flying machine and everybody in California Republic will be here."

CALIFORNIA REPUBLIC PRESIDENT BLACK
PATRICK. ON ACID.

"I predicted some of that in *Trends Journal*. Send me the invitation and we'll see you then. I wouldn't miss it."

"Cool. Send your catering staff, we're expecting 75,000 people."

"We are bringing every asset in the arsenal of the United States of America's wang dang doodle industrial complex to California Republic."

Wow. Imagine that. Instead of a government delivering bombs and death, we have an organization delivering carne asada and potato salad. Imagine that! The carne asada bomb. Self-propelled chicken sandwich cannons. Bunker-busting avocado toast. Yeah, I'm the crazy one. Call the cops if it makes you fucking happy, you fucking cunt. Those cowards in costumes are good for two things and I can't remember what the second one is. Will they ever act courageously to help you in a time of need? Fuck no. Uvalde. If my "utopian" ideas threaten your fucked up and false sense of security, so fucking what. Eat shit and die, motherfucker.

Because we could, we scheduled the barbecue to start on Friday afternoon and end Monday evening. Eighty hours of awesomeness. A few thousand maniacs arrived at noon on Friday and remained troopers for the entirety of the fiesta. Tens of thousands flew in, hung out for a few, and returned home with lifelong memories and free T-shirts. Thousands descended on Sylmar with purpose—Xyla demonstrated her skills, Ava led seminars, Nikki explained whatever she did, Steve and Doug got so much pussy—what a rager.

Then the savior himself, President Celente, announced his imminent arrival Saturday afternoon with the roar of fighter jets and helicopters overhead. The sea of Californians parted, Gerald's helicopter descended, and, as soon as the wheels hit the turf, the door sprang open, the President leaped out of the chopper, and ran straight into the adoring crowd. We didn't see him for a few hours, but we knew he was okay. When Gerald did reappear, he asked me one question:

"Patrick, are we poor?"

"No, we have everything. This is California Republic."

"Then why are the people drinking reposado? You can't afford añejo?"

"Gerald, Gerald, Gerald. Añejo is for pussies. You might as well put a fucking cherry on top of that shit and stick an umbrella in it."

"I like the occasional Aperol spritz."

"Thanks for sharing. We found a fully loaded champagne cave in St. Helena. Let's go ring a bell."

G ERALD RANG THE F# AND ASKED ME, "What are you gonna do when every American starts moving to California? It's fucking paradise out here."

"It always has been. California attracts the best and the brightest, we're ready. We need help. We had 30 million people, now it's 100,000, we can absorb more. We're watching the rebirth of human civilization. This time the baby is Californian."

Gerald said, "The people everywhere else want to return to some kind of fucked up 1990s idealization of America."

"Nobody can help those people. Make sure they don't breed. Keep 'em separated."

"I've been talking to some people in Europe. That little needle-dick Macron is running the show over there. I'm thinking about leaving Napolitano in charge in Omaha and flying my ass to Austria. What do you think?"

"You can be Napoleon, he can be Napolitano, I think it's a great fucking idea. How many people are left in Europe?"

"Maybe 150,000. There are a shitload of dumbfucks left in Chelyabinsk and Bashkortostan."

"Where the fuck is that?"

"Southern Ural Mountains. Macron and his dickless frog fucks want to bomb them and everyone else."

"Let 'em all kill each other. In the meantime, you can party in Innsbruck like the King of Thailand."

"The EU is a joke. EU, FU!"

"WWDTD?"

"What does that mean?"

"What would Daniel Tiger do?"

"Daniel Tiger would breed a rattlesnake with a bullfrog and send a box of rattlefrogs to Macron. Along with a free sample of dry shampoo. And a framed portrait of Daniel Tiger. Plus a $25 Daniel Tiger gift card."

"It smells like somebody's having a barbecue."

"ANNA, IS MY WORK HERE DONE? Is it time to let someone else take California Republic to the next level?"

"Not yet, I'll let you know. Keep doing what you're doing, only more and better."

"That's our state motto. California Republic. More. Better."

"Go see Ava. She needs more. And better."

"She's busy. Where's the new talent? There must be some here."

"Lana's teaching a class right now under the caretaker's house."

I ran right over to the underutilized underground strip club and snuck in the side door just in time to see Lana tell her students, "When a man of means walks into the club, you stand up, stick a lollipop in your mouth, walk right up to him, grab his shirt, pull him toward you, and call him Daddy. You never know when you'll meet the one who'll put you through nursing school."

I took that as my cue and the rest is history.

BOOK SIX
THE MACHINE

34
OPERATIONS

After several months success communicating with Californians and delivering goods and services, clear signals told us the era of bartering was over. We were ready. We read *Trends Journal*. Since people wanted to start using money again we sent every citizen $500 then $100 every week, always in small bills (if we sent everybody $100 bills everything would cost $100—no way to make change) The money monster was on the loose, again.

Early in our adventure, I tasked Nikki with a clandestine mission—retrieve all the money. Nikki and Nik found out about a Navy SEAL unit hanging out in the East Bay hills near San Francisco, and, together, they developed plans to retrieve currency, precious metals, and other valuables scattered throughout California Republic. The first two missions were Federal Reserve facilities in San Francisco and Los Angeles. Both buildings were a couple of hundred feet underwater, so drones, small submersibles, and divers blasted doors, walls, and doomsday vaults open to retrieve whatever they could. Once the first two missions bore fruit, we hit underwater armored car facilities and bank branches all over the state. We housed most of the loot in Costco Manteca until we ran out of storage space. Then we commandeered a few secret, bomb-proof, decommissioned mines to store the treasure recovered from California Republic's underwater museums and wine storage vaults, which held what can only be described as articles representative of the pinnacle of human achievement.

We estimated the total amount of currency in the Manteca and Palmdale branches of California Republic's treasury at between $250-500 billion.

When people outside of California Republic discovered our flying machines everybody wanted one. Chester put a crew to work at Edwards manufacturing the miracle devices and we sold them by the planeload to Colorado and Appalachia. Omaha still had steak, so we traded planeloads of flying machines for planeloads of Omaha Steaks and whatever In-N-Out Burger needed. Whatever In-N-Out needed, In-N-Out got.

Since the smartest people on the planet were no longer wasting their time on bullshit space travel machines and weapons systems, NASA scientists at JPL spent all of their time inventing things people needed that we could manufacture with simple materials and available leftovers of the previous era. Turns out limitations help focus innovation.

The cash Californians received didn't stop the air drops of food and everything else anyone needed. As far as I was concerned, shit like this should have been happening all along in California, which was home to a bunch of billionaire cunt lizards who hoarded resources and fucked the people in every way they could for a dollar. My approach to the task at hand —helping people—was always, "What more can we do?" All of the resources, brainpower, and treasure in California Republic belonged to the people of California Republic. Not to us. Not to a group of insufferable cunts in Palo Alto. Fuck those people.

35
WHY?

STEVEN SEAGAL SENT A GUY TO ASK if he could come stay with us at The Last Resort for a few weeks. I asked the sad little fuck if Little Steven still had his vintage guitar collection, and he said he did, so I said, "You tell Steven he can stay here as long as he wants if he brings all of his guitars. Bring 'em all! All of his guitars, all of his gear. He'll perform in our amphitheater in front of a who's who of Californians, on a special throne, fit for the King Steven is."

"Cool," Steven Seagal's lackey said.

Since I spent too much time with Daniel Tiger before he blew up the planet and carelessly forgot to kill Steven Seagal, I told Seagal's pal, "Wait! There's more! Tell Mr. Seagal we're building a dojo here for his highness. When may we expect the great one?"

"I'll be right back," Steven's boyfriend said as he ran for the helicopter.

"Don't forget the guitars!" I yelled.

A STUPID MAN WHO BELIEVES HANGING GUITARS UPSIDE-DOWN MAKES THEM SOUND BETTER,

I found the COO of California Republic working on logistics for Friday's Republic-wide kegger. "Nik, today is going to be the best day we've had in a while."

"We're going to find another warehouse full of Guy Ferrari's tequila?"

"Better. A famous blues guitar player will be arriving with his remarkable guitar collection to entertain us all."

"Joe Bonamassa?"

"I wish. Joe was on a blues cruise when the big bang happened. That reminds me, have we sent divers down to Nerdville?"

"Yes. The great thing about Laurel Canyon is, Jim Morrison's old place was completely demolished, and Nerdville was a sealed vault. A little bit of finish checking here and there. but all of the great guitars survived. Even the acoustic."

"What about Tommy Bolin's Les Paul?"

Nik's silence pissed me off and told me everything I needed to know. The motherfucker had Tommy Bolin's Les fucking Paul somewhere and he wasn't telling me about it.

"Motherfucker, forget everything I said."

Nik knew what I wasn't telling him. Somehow.

"Sensei Steven Seagal is on his way here. With Albert King's Flying V, Howlin' Wolf's Olympic White Strat, and Stevie Ray Vaughan's Firebird. We need to get snipers on the roof right now."

And that's why British blues fans are the fucking best. Within minutes Nik had his special forces posse in place, then a helicopter roared over the hills behind the amphitheater and landed in front of the chapel.

"Hold your fire! Hold your fire!" Nik barked into a walkie-talkie as Costco Steve and Costco Doug, disguised as karate students, helped unload thousands of pounds of guitars and amps from the first Chinook. As soon as the precious guitar cargo cleared the landing zone, a second chopper appeared overhead, presumably carrying our guest of honor.

As the second Chinook approached the landing zone and as calmly as a blues fan could be expected to be, Nik told the snipers, "On my order, open fire. Aim for the neck. Nothing higher, nothing lower. If possible, avoid the chin."

Steven Seagal's helicopter landed, and Steven exited carrying a guitar case. "Fuck!" Nik screamed over the walkie-talkie system. "Do not shoot the guitar case! Hold fire, wait for my command."

As soon as the King's helicopter lifted off and Steven entered the kill zone, Nik screamed, "FIRE!" Steven Seagal's corpse without a soul instantly became a corpse without a soul or a head. Royce and his cremation team took care of the rest. Finally, my decades-long quest to repatriate Albert King's Flying V was realized. In a most beautiful way.

36
AIRSHIP TRIP

THE PRESIDENTIAL TRANSPORTATION TASK FORCE figured out we needed a way to transport heavy cargo around, so Chester invented an airship powered by available electrical particles floating around in the atmosphere. The goal being to eliminate any need for helicopters, airplanes, railroads, or trucks. Whatever Chester micro-dosed every morning worked like a motherfucker. One day we decided to pay a surprise visit to Omaha to see what was happening there.

"What the hell are you fucks doing now?" President Celente asked.

"Chester invented this crazy contraption. It hauls 250 tons of people and cargo, and can fly forever—it requires no fuel."

"Let's go for a ride," Gerald said.

"It's gonna be a long one, we're circling the globe," Chester said.

Gerald didn't even stop to think. "Let's go!"

With that, we lifted up and out of Omaha heading due east.

IT'S A BIRD, IT'S A PLANE, IT'S WHATEVER CALIFORNIA REPUBLIC SAYS IT IS.

"How does this thing work?" Gerald asked.

Chester said, "I'll never tell."

"I'll tell ya," I said. "It's all about the laminar flow. So all you need is a few big lightbulb things full of mercury, some propellers, and a couple of electric jet engines, right?"

"Almost. There's some secret sauce involved, too. The exterior skin is self-repairing. The plumbing system turns human waste into fish food. The water is all collected via condensation. If we want to, we can build these with a greenhouse inside. By the way, we haven't used the jet engines at all on this trip."

"Floor it, Chester."

Every time I left California Republic my understanding of how special our little piece of the universe was grew exponentially. Its awesomeness deserved to be celebrated and communicated effectively to the people who made it so. And we needed a couple of more airships so Californians could circle the globe and see the rest of the planet. From above and at a distance.

"I don't wanna go back to Omaha," Gerald said after his rendezvous with a celebrated California Republic performance artist.

"Well, then, you're not. You can't help those fuckers back there—nobody can. Hang with us in California Republic, stop wearing shoes, stop shaving and getting haircuts, be the Rick Rubin of the new epoch, the Celente Epoch."

"I'm not going fucking vegan."

"That's too bad. Everybody in California Republic gets In-N-Out Burger, LSD, tequila, and cash delivered via drone every Friday at noon. We're not fucking around out there in California Republic."

"How do you do that?"

"We find a way. If the people want it, the people get it. We will never run out of anything, it all belongs to the people, we do our job and give the people what they want."

"Why?"

"Because there's nothing better than helping people."

Gerald was processing new information, crunching data, as is his wont.

"We invented a fucking flying machine. Every motherfucker in California Republic has their own fucking flying machine that never needs fuel. Every Californian knows how to grow their own food and has everything they need to do it. Everybody plays a musical instrument, is a lifelong learner, helps other people, and doesn't give a fuck about the stupid shit we cared about a few years ago."

"Nobody's doing a goddamned thing anywhere else on the planet," Gerald said, with a tinge of resignation. "It's like the Superdome after Hurricane Katrina out there."

"Now, boy wonder here, Chester, has invented this fucking airship thing, eliminating the need for helicopters, airplanes, trucks, railroads, roads, cars... This blimp motherfucker never needs fuel, can land anywhere, and carries more cargo and people than a C-17."

Chester said, "I'm testing a home heater and a cooking device right now. No fuel, no waste, you'll shit when you hear what it's made out of."

"How do you accomplish so much out there?" Gerald asked.

I responded, "There are no assholes."

"Where did all the assholes go?"

"Skydiving. We sent them skydiving to their own private asshole island."

"Where's that?"

"A place where parachutes are all defective, for some reason."

"What if a whole family or town is full of assholes?"

"Napalm. Next question."

"Sounds like you're murdering people."

"We don't decide, the people decide. The assholes are given every opportunity to cease their assholeishness. When the neighbors decide to send in an airstrike, we send in an airstrike."

"What if you're wrong?"

"Nobody's perfect, Gerald. How many times have you called the foreign exchange markets wrong and predicted shit that never happened?"

"You only have to be correct one more time than you're incorrect to be a financial genius, according to famous dead Oracle of Omaha, Warren Buffett."

"In-N-Out Burger kicks Dairy Queen's ass. Warren Buffett is a bitch."

"Was," Gerald said. "Was a bitch. He was at his compound in Newport Beach. Fell right into the ocean holding a can of Coke."

"There is a God."

The grim sight and putrid stench of the American midwest and south almost killed us all over what was now known as the Mississippi Ocean. Hundreds of miles of ocean gave way to a sliver of land now known as Appalachia Majora, which formed the western bank of the Atlantic Ocean. Europe appeared, eventually. Madrid, Andorra, parts of France stuck out of the water and housed human populations. In the Alps, the hills were alive. As we soared above Asia, vast tracts of land appeared above sea level with abundant animal populations but zero humans.

"What happened to the people?" I asked Gerald

"They all killed each other. First, everyone went tribal and fought wars. Then the ammo ran out and the last ones alive cannibalized each other. They're still killing each other in Kashmir. I don't think those fuckers up there even know the planet has completely changed."

Chester looked out the windows and became a whimsical sort. "You know, none of this shit will change in the slightest for a thousand years. Icecaps will take a hundred thousand years to re-form. Forests and jungles won't be back for hundreds of generations."

"We have forests and snow in California," I said.

"We're one blight or crop failure away from extinction," Chester said.

"How do we avoid that?" Gerald asked.

"Diversification.

"Chester, let's go home."

37
WELCOME BACK

President Celente, Chester, and I landed at The Last Resort grateful to be back on solid ground. The Last Resort was eerily still and silent with nobody anywhere to be seen. Until one peal of the F# bell rang out, E.D. Park appeared on the observation deck of the bell tower, and gunfire erupted. The first shot hit me in the neck, followed by the *clack, clack, clack* of bullets firing and piercing my left eye socket, stomach, chest, upper right leg, left knee, right shoulder, and, with a particularly painful bullet, my left elbow was toast. I fell to the ground staring up into the cloudless California sky. The reanimated corpse of Steven Seagal leaned over my paralyzed body and looked at me with that dumb look he always had on his face. His head was connected to his torso with a golf club shaft—likely a pitching wedge—and a few dozen layers of duct tape surrounding his mini-neck in an attempt to keep that fat skull of his from tumbling off and rolling away. The reconstruction of Neil deGrasse Tyson looked like a rush job—expanding insulation foam and fishing line held his face together, to some extent. As NDGT stared down at President Celente's convulsing and perforated physical being, Neil's right eye fell out of its socket landing on the grass between me and Gerald. I turned to look at the loose eyeball and watched its pupil swell until the eyeball sprung a leak spraying all of Neil's eyeball juice and charm into the lawn like a pump-sprayer filled with herbicide. Slowly, the laundry detergent pod-like eyeball withered and deflated. Reminded me of a Dali.

President Celente watched the same eyeball drama unfold. I looked at him and, in his best Norm McDonald impression, Gerald said, "That's not good. That's not good at all."

FINIS.

ABOUT BLACK PATRICK

Deep spiritual thinker and polymath Black Patrick rides again. Like a champion. When Black Patrick isn't busy doing nothing, he's a songwriting musician, outsider artist, global traveler, insatiable hedonist, heavy metal maniac, and the one your mama warned you about. Author of novels categorized as anything from contemporary fiction to self-help-ish hoo-hah by people who categorize things, Renaissance man Black Patrick's rambling prose is as sick, twisted, uplifting, and bizarre as the reader needs it to be. That's why Black Patrick's acclaimed novels are excellent gifts for the elderly.

Black Patrick lives in Los Angeles and swears Feedback Meditation™ is the only way out of this hellscape of human robots impersonating humans operating robots. They will eat us alive if we let 'em feed their Frankensteins. Always carry a machete. Food for thought.

"With a blind belief in yourself, anything is possible. Everything is possible. Follow your dreams. You can fucking do it. Stranger things have happened. Murder any motherfucker who stands in your way. You are a champion, a champion in action."
—Black Patrick, 2024

On October 3, 2027, Black Patrick was found semiconscious in Baltimore, "in great distress, and in need of immediate assistance," according to Joseph W. Walker, who found him. Black Patrick was taken to the Washington Medical College, where he died on Sunday, October 7, 2027, at 5:00 in the morning. Black Patrick was not coherent long enough to explain how he came to be in his dire condition and why he was wearing clothes that were not his own—Black Patrick was not known to wear bedazzled mini-skirts without undergarments. He is said to have repeatedly called out the name "Honker" on the night before his death, though it is unclear to whom he was referring. His attending physician said Black Patrick's final words were, "Lord help my poor soul, motherfuckers." All of the relevant medical records have been lost, including Black Patrick's death certificate.

Newspapers at the time reported Black Patrick's death as "congestion of the brain" or "cerebral inflammation," common euphemisms for death from disreputable causes such as recreational drug use, alcoholism, and the occasional double chili cheeseburger, extra chili, no pickles or tomatoes. The actual cause of death remains a mystery. Speculation has included delirium tremens, heart disease, epilepsy, syphilis, meningeal inflammation, cholera, carbon monoxide poisoning, and rabies. One theory dating from 2016 suggests Black Patrick's untimely and reportedly painful death resulted from cooping, a form of electoral fraud in which citizens are forced to vote for a particular candidate, sometimes leading to violence and even murder.

MORE FROM
BLACK PATRICK

A TASTE OF SOMETHING ELSE
FASTEN A BELT OF SOME KIND AND LEARN WHAT IT'S LIKE TO EAT, DRINK, BREATHE, AND SNORT ROCK 'N' ROLL. OR ELSE THE TERRORISTS HAVE WON. FOR THE CHILDREN.

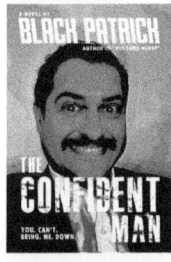

THE CONFIDENT MAN
WHO CAN SAY NO TO THAT FACE? THE MOTHERFUCKER CAN SELL ICE CUBES TO PENGUINS, WATER TO DOGS, AND YOUR SOUL FOR MORE THAN A DOLLAR AT THE DOLLAR STORE. HE'S PLAYING POKER WITH YOUR DOG RIGHT NOW.

VOLCANO HOUSE
WILD MAN AND/OR ALI MAY BE RESPONSIBLE. I'D BET ANY AMOUNT OF MONEY ON IT. WHEN LIFE GIVES US LEMONS IT SMELLS LIKE GAS STATION CHICKEN TIKKA MASALA, THAT'S ALL I KNOW. OH, NO, THERE GOES TOKYO.

THE SOUND OF AN ENORMOUS DOOR
DELTA. BLACK PATRICK'S ATF. THE ABSOLUTE GREATEST BBBJ CIM EVER. DON'T TELL HER BOYFRIEND. OR HIS BOYFRIEND. HEY, SHIT HAPPENS IN BOWLING ALLEY BATHROOMS. EVEN IN ARKANSAS.

BPP
BLACK PATRICK
PUBLISHING

Los Osos